BOYS IN HEAT

BOYS IN HEAT

GAY EROTIC STORIES

EDITED BY
RICHARD LABONTÉ

CLEIS PRESS

Cleis Press Inc., P.O. Box 14697, San Francisco, California 94114
Printed in the United States.

Cover design: Scott Idleman
Cover photograph: Celesta Danger
Text design: Frank Wiedemann
Cleis logo art: Juana Alicia
First Edition.
10 9 8 7 6 5 4 3 2 1

"Duffle" © 2008 by Dallas Angguish. "Miss Vel's Place" © 2008 by Jonathan Asche. "Burning the Midnight Oil" © 2008 by Michael Cain. "Fluid Mechanics" © 2008 by Dale Chase. "A Recipe For..." © 2008 by Kal Cobalt. "The Key-Maker's Wife" © 2008 by Ted Cornwell. "Talking to Mr. Mack" © 2008 by Thomas Fuchs. "Intimacy" © 2008 by Drew Gummerson. "Telling a Switch's Story" © 2008 by Arden Hill. "Burlington" © 2008 by Phillip Mackenzie, Jr. "Unmasked" © 2008 by Syd McGinley. "Cockfighting" © 2008 by Keith Peck. "Three Scenes" © 2008 by Christopher Schmidt. "Hooking Up" © 2006 by J. M. Snyder, reprinted with permission from *Shorts* (Lulu Press, 2006). "The Manor" © 2008 by Andrew Warburton. "Orbs" © 2008 by Clarence Wong.

For Asa Dean Noble,
noble new name, same fine man

Contents

ix *Introduction* • Richard Labonté

1   *A Recipe For...* • Kal Cobalt
17   *Hooking Up* • J. M. Snyder
30   *Cockfighting* • Keith Peck
47   *Duffle* • Dallas Angguish
61   *Miss Vel's Place* • Jonathan Asche
74   *Orbs* • Clarence Wong
87   *Intimacy* • Drew Gummerson
107 *Burning the Midnight Oil* • Michael Cain
113 *Fluid Mechanics* • Dale Chase
122 *Talking to Mr. Mack* • Thomas Fuchs
133 *The Key-Maker's Wife* • Ted Cornwell
142 *Telling a Switch's Story* • Arden Hill
145 *The Manor* • Andrew Warburton
158 *Three Scenes* • Christopher Schmidt
164 *Unmasked* • Syd McGinley
172 *Burlington* • Phillip Mackenzie, Jr.

185 *About the Authors*
190 *About the Editor*

| INTRODUCTION

B oys rubbing together: ignition is inevitable, and always desirable, as the profound pleasure of friction kicks in.

For some, like the nervous surfer boy in Dallas Angguish's "Duffle," fleeing his harshly religious family for the liberating haven of university—and the bed, finally, of his older brother's pal—it's a scary new experience; for the virgin in Jonathan Asche's "Miss Vel's Place," discovering he can pop his cherry with the help of a brothel's male caretaker is a welcome relief. For the Internet boys in J. M. Snyder's "Hooking Up," it's a grand adventure spiced with the uncertainty of matching a webcam face to a real body. And for the cocksure kid in Michael Cain's "Burning the Midnight Oil," with a jizz-filled monster in his pants yearning for release, seduction of a fellow student is what the game is all about.

For others, sexual excitement is a way of life: the cum contest in Keith Peck's "Cockfighting" presents boys playing hard—really, really hard; the gay couple in Syd McGinley's "Unmasked" add zest to their sex with some Halloween shenanigans; and one of the freewheeling buddies on a road trip in Phillip Mackenzie, Jr.'s "Burlington" delights in picking up an eager boy-toy along the way for a fling; that love-'em-and-leave-'em style is what Kal Cobalt's "A Recipe For..." is all about as well; and when an Asian teacher/waiter meets a pierced Aussie adventurer on a San Diego nude beach in Clarence Wong's "Orbs," sparks fly.

Teachers and students go at it in Dale Chase's "Fluid Mechanics" and Andrew Warburton's "The Manor," two tales that get inside the heads of their characters, adding a dash of darkness to the flame of passion. In Thomas Fuchs' "Talking to Mr. Mack," an older man avidly absorbs the stories of hot sex recounted by the hooker he's hired for an afternoon; in Ted Cornwell's "The Key-Maker's Wife," a smitten underemployed young man discovers, to his explosive relief, that the married man he's been lusting after for weeks isn't all that straight; and Drew Gummerson conjures a harsh eastern European milieu where two military men connect sexually while tracking a serial killer in the tender "Intimacy."

Rounding out the collection are two tales that forsake linear storytelling—but not sex. Arden Hill, in "Telling a Switch's Story," gets inside the head of a bottom with a top's tendencies, and Christopher Schmidt, in "Three Scenes," considers cruising other boys when the boyfriend's away, plays nimbly with the word *fuck,* and dwells on butt.

Boys in Heat...that's what this book is all about, from playful erotic encounters to muscular carnal sex.

Richard Labonté
Bowen Island, British Columbia

A RECIPE FOR...

Kal Cobalt

For M.P.

Y ou can find your way home, right?" Scott yelled. I didn't hear him so much as read his lips while the club's dance music pummeled my eardrums. In the flashes of strobe light, I saw that Scott's previously perfectly coiffed hair had fallen down over his forehead and at least two buttons of his dress shirt had come undone.

"Yeah," I yelled back, and nodded in case he hadn't heard me. It might have been my first night in the big city, but I knew that Scott's abrupt absence from the dance floor for the last ten minutes plus his debauched look and frantic kiss-off equaled imminent sex at somebody else's apartment. I was already throwing Scott off his game by staying at his place. Dragging him outside so we could have a conversation about the best way for me to get back home seemed unconscionable on top of that. It couldn't be that hard to hail a cab.

Twenty minutes later, I was hopelessly lost. I'd headed toward what had looked like the flashing lights of more popular clubs on a main thoroughfare, only to discover that they'd been reflections of police cruiser lights on the cracked panes of an abandoned storefront. Streetlights became less frequent, and when I could see the sidewalk under my feet I saw other things I would rather not have—spent condoms, used syringes. I had no sense of which direction would get me out of the bad side of town the quickest, and then, as if to punish me for my ineptitude, it started to rain. I didn't even have a hood on my jacket, let alone an umbrella. I hadn't yet replaced the cell phone my ex took when I moved away, and the neighborhood seemed conspicuously cleansed of pay phones.

Two men rounded a corner ahead of me and headed in my direction, engaged in a harsh, profanity-laced debate. Shoving my hands deep into my pockets to protect them from the rain, I ducked into the nearest alley, figuring nothing could lurk there that was scarier than getting involved in the shoving match coming my way. If they followed me into the alley, I decided, I'd just turn around and hand them my wallet and watch before they asked for it. Try to save us all a little trouble.

Halfway down the alley, there was a lone dim light, and beneath it, the glare of a cigarette's ember. As I got closer, I could make out the man who was smoking: tall and scrawny, wearing a white, food-stained apron underneath a black leather jacket. He had close-cropped salt-and-pepper hair and deep, hard eyes. He gave me a jerky little half-nod and said, "Hey."

"Hey," I said, and glanced behind me to make sure the arguing men weren't following.

The man in the apron took a deep drag off his cigarette. "Lost?"

I grinned sheepishly. "It's that obvious?"

He gave me a long, appraising look, and abruptly I wished I'd met him in a club instead of an alley. "Yeah," he said. "Not from the city, are you?"

"No. I mean, I am now. I mean, I just moved here, today." The rain began to seep through my jacket, and I couldn't suppress a shudder.

He raised an eyebrow. "You're running around the city unsupervised? That doesn't seem wise."

I felt my face flush. "It's a long story."

He grunted, then took another drag.

"Listen," I said. "If you have a phone I could use, I'd really appreciate it. I just need a cab back to where I'm staying."

"Where's that?"

"With a friend."

"No, I mean where's the place?"

I searched my pockets for Scott's business card. I'd written his home address on the back. "I have it here somewhere."

He sighed. "What neighborhood?"

"I don't know," I confessed, searching my pockets again. "It took us about thirty minutes to get to the club but I've been walking for almost that long, and I'm all turned around."

He shook his head. "Jesus. Well, come on inside, warm up a little at least." He crushed out his cigarette and opened the door behind him.

"Thank you." I stepped inside, blinking in surprise at what I saw. I'd understood he was a cook, but somehow I hadn't quite expected to find myself inside a darkened professional kitchen, all stainless steel and white tile.

"Office is in here." He led the way, plopping a giant telephone book on the cluttered desk. "Maybe you'll get lucky and your friend has a listed address."

"Yeah. Thanks." I thumbed through the book, trying to

ignore my shaking hands. I wasn't that wet, just miserably cold and unable to warm up thanks to the dampness.

"Here." He turned on a space heater and nudged it toward me with his foot before lighting up another cigarette.

"God, thank you." I turned my chair to take full advantage of the heat, resting the phone book on my lap, and soon found Scott's listing, complete with address.

Immediately, the cook was on the phone, not bothering to remove the cigarette from his mouth. He identified himself as what sounded like "Jaiben," read off Scott's address, and asked how long. Within thirty seconds flat, he was off the phone again. "Cab'll be here in about five."

"Thank you. I really can't thank you enough." I shifted in front of the space heater again, trying to at least leach the dampness out of my jeans.

"No problem," he said, watching the way I moved around in the chair. "Smoke?"

"No, thank you."

"Shame," he said, exhaling a plume. "Warms you up fast."

I laughed a little. "Well, if I find myself spending a lot of nights lost in this kind of weather, I'll consider taking it up."

"You really do need a keeper," he told me. "The way you look, you should be glad you weren't mugged in this neighborhood."

I looked down at myself, at my best attempt to dress properly for a night of clubbing. "I tried," I pointed out fruitlessly.

He shook his head. "It's not the way you're dressed. It's the whole package. You've got that small-town farm-raised wholesome boy thing going on. Innocence and fear in equal measures. Lotta people in this town'll take advantage of that."

"Well, thank you for not being one of them," I said, unsure how else to reply.

He smiled at me. "People who don't take advantage of you have their reasons."

Before I could ask what he meant, the phone rang, and he gestured toward the door. "Go around the front. Your cab's waiting."

I stood up and extended my hand. "Thank you for all your help."

He shook my hand firmly, his eyes steady on mine. "You're welcome."

"And then what happened?" Scott asked, shaking Tabasco into his Bloody Mary at an alarming rate.

"And then nothing, I got in the cab and came home and went to bed."

Scott shook his head. "You didn't come on to him?"

"He just called me a cab and let me get warm."

"That's my point."

"What was I supposed to do, ask him to share the cab?"

"That would've been good. Obviously, he was at the end of his shift, he had to get home somehow, right?"

"Wouldn't he have gone home however he got there? In his car or something?"

Scott sipped his drink. "You're overthinking. Pickup lines don't have to make sense."

"I don't even know if he was gay."

"He had to be. He stayed with you all that time, made small talk."

I shrugged. "Back home, people are just friendly like that."

"Back home, everybody knew you. They weren't friendly like that once they found out why you were getting divorced, were they?"

That hurt. "That's not fair, Scott."

"I'm not trying to be mean, I'm just saying. Small towns operate differently. You're either in the fold or outside it. In the city, usually attraction is a prerequisite to otherwise-unmotivated generosity."

That sounded ugly to me, but at the same time, I liked the idea that the cook had been interested in me—I'd certainly felt an attraction. "Well, what do I do now?"

Scott shook his head. "You go back, of course."

"What am I supposed to do, just walk into the kitchen?"

Scott looked at me as if I were pathetic. "You really are clueless, aren't you? You go to the restaurant and tell them you're looking for a cook who worked last night and you describe him."

"What, tonight?"

"Do you think you'll have better luck waiting a month? Yes, tonight."

Just the thought of that—of walking into a restaurant and asking a total stranger to find someone I was attracted to—made my stomach shudder. "Will you come with me?"

"That pretty much defeats the purpose. You want him to know you're single."

"What if he's not there?"

"What if you break your leg on the way? Don't borrow trouble."

"I don't even know what I'd do if I saw him again."

Scott rolled his eyes. "You'd say, 'Hi, I want to thank you for your help last night. Can I treat you to a drink after your shift?' "

"How do you know to say stuff like that?"

"Five years in the city."

"Well, what if he's not interested?"

"Then he'll say something like 'Thanks, but that's not necessary, and I have to get some sleep,' and you nod and say something like 'Okay, well, thanks again, I'll see you around sometime,' and you steal some flatware and you go home."

"Scott!" I laughed despite myself. "I'm not going to steal from him."

"I'm just saying, you suck it up. That's all. You have no practice in sucking it up."

"Okay, okay. I even know his name, or I sort of do. That'll probably help."

"What do you mean, you sort of do?"

"Well, it sounded sort of like 'Jaiben.' "

Scott blinked. "How far the fuck did you walk?"

"What?"

"How far the fuck did you walk? Oh, holy fucking shit." Scott set down his Bloody Mary and raked both hands through his unruly hair. "Oh my fucking god."

"Scott, this isn't funny."

"You have a hard-on for J. Benjamin of J. Benjamin Bistro. Holy shit." Scott blinked at me. "If he screws you, you have to ask for his truffle torte recipe. Please?"

By the time I got up the nerve to walk through the front doors of J. Benjamin Bistro, I was a wreck. Scott had shown me my crush's photograph in the paper, the four-star review of the restaurant, the astronomically priced "Chef's choice" menu. If I'd harbored any hope of the cook being in my league, the show-and-tell from Scott's scrapbook dashed it.

An impeccably dressed hostess gave me a big but professional smile. "Good evening. Are you meeting a party?"

"No. I'm—well, sort of. I was hoping to talk to Mr. Benjamin for a second."

Her smile widened. "I'm sorry, sir, but Mr. Benjamin is working in the kitchen this evening and is unavailable. Do you have a business card I can give to him?"

"Uh. No." Of course he was busy with the dinner rush. I couldn't help feeling a little angry at Scott; he would have known that, should have stopped me from making a fool of myself. "I was just—I got lost last night and he helped me, and I wanted to thank him."

"Oh!" She gave me a more sincere smile then. "He told me that story. It was very sweet." She favored me with a conspiratorial little look. "Would you like to have a seat and I'll see if he knows when he might be available?"

"That would be great. Thank you." I dropped into the chair before my knees gave out. I couldn't even begin to reason out what his storytelling meant.

Soon the hostess was back, still smiling. "It's a very busy night, but if you have time, he'd like you to have a snack on the house and join him once things slow down enough for him to take a break."

I managed a stunned smile. "Thank you, that would be—I don't have anywhere else to be."

She escorted me to a small table in a corner. Within moments, I had a tall glass of water and an elegant little plate of cheese and fruit before me. I nibbled, trying not to freak out.

Half an hour later, the hostess led me back to the kitchen, where half a dozen cooks worked feverishly over stovetops and counters. "J. Ben?" she called.

"Hey." He came around the center island, and I lost my breath. Even without the leather jacket, the attraction was still there; the apron clung to his slender frame, and sweat darkened the roots of his hair.

"Hi," I said. "Um—I didn't mean to bother you."

"No bother. I'm going out for a cigarette." He jerked his head toward the door. "C'mon."

I followed him out to the alley, which didn't look nearly as intimidating in the twilight. "I guess I don't know why I'm here," I stammered. "I just wanted to thank you for helping me. I wanted you to know I got home okay."

He leaned back against the alley wall, smirking as he took out his cigarettes. "And got back here okay, too."

"Well…yeah." I felt like a complete dork. How had I failed to realize that he was far too experienced to be interested in me? "You really didn't have to send free food—I should pay you for that. I came to say thank you, you don't owe me anything."

He breathed a cigarette to life, waving off my concern. "Don't worry about it. I was glad you came back."

"You were? I mean, you are?"

He smiled. "Sure."

"Mr. Benjamin, I—"

"Nah. Ben."

I swallowed. "Ben. I came back because, uh…" I swallowed again. All I could think was that he would laugh at me, embarrass me, send me away. "I don't know if you're…interested or even if you go this way, but…"

Ben breathed out smoke. "But you're coming on to me anyway?"

Mortified, I just nodded.

He nodded back. "I'm usually done around one. You feel like meeting me here, I'll take you to the chef bar."

I blinked. "Chef bar?"

"Late-night hangout where those of us with nocturnal jobs hang out. Seedy. Hope that's not a problem." He gave me a firm, sizing-up look that embarrassed and attracted me all at once.

"Not a problem," I managed. "I'll be here at one."

He nodded. "Good." He looked at me again. "Get some rest."

After incessant teasing from Scott and a bout of nerves so severe I thought I'd have to stay home just to remain near the bathroom, I finally managed to make it back to the alley and wait. I'd nearly given up when Ben stepped out the door at one-thirty, dressed in jeans and a white T-shirt under his leather jacket, cigarette already dangling from his lips. "Let's go," he said.

I followed a pace behind him, trying not to stare at his ass—and then I realized that was probably the whole point. His jacket was cut a little long, but that was alluring in itself, giving me a reason to watch as the hem swayed from one side to the other with every step.

He wasn't kidding about the seediness of the bar. As he shoved open the door, a loud blast of last year's dance music assaulted my ears. The floor—what I could see of it in the dim light—looked like it hadn't been cleaned in months. People in various stages of dress and inebriation sprawled on stained couches, some necking, some on the verge of passing out. Ben grinned through it all, weaving his way through the insanity to the bar.

"Two Heinekens," he said, ordering for us both, and then passed one off to me before heading further into the club. Toward the back of the club was a doorway with a curtain drawn across it. Ben made a beeline for it.

I knew about back rooms. I'd noticed that this bar leaned toward straight, though, and so I wasn't really sure what to expect. I followed Ben as closely as I could, afraid to lose track of him in a place so foreign to me.

It wasn't quite the kind of back room Scott might have liked. I almost choked on the density of cigarette smoke, so hazy that it took my eyes a moment to adjust. There was a universal cry of "Ben!" from a dozen men sprawled out on yet more of the ubiquitous couches that had seen better days. "Who's that?" one added, and I felt my face flush at the attention.

"My date," Ben replied. He gripped the back of my neck and piloted me to the nearest unoccupied couch.

A lot of kitchen stories were told, but I don't remember the specifics. Ben kept his hand on me the entire time, squeezing the back of my neck, rubbing down my spine, carding his fingers through the hair at the back of my head. I was so hard I ached, but I could still barely stand to even look at him beside me, afraid of somehow ruining the casual affection.

As a heavyset man settled into a long tale involving something about fifty covers and a busted stove, Ben nuzzled the side of my neck, smelling me before placing a kiss just below my ear. I whimpered softly, closing my eyes. It was embarrassing to be touched like that in front of so many people, even if they didn't seem to notice. Ben placed a hand on my cheek and turned my face toward his, then kissed me hard, thrusting his tongue into my mouth immediately. He tasted of stale cigarettes and fresh beer, and I thought my cock would tear right through the fly of my slacks.

"You wanna get out of here?" he murmured, resting a hand so high up on my thigh that my cock jumped.

"Yes, please," I breathed, grateful that he didn't seem to need anything more cogent from me.

He stood and said his good-byes, and aside from a couple of catcalls there was no comment about our necking. He put his hand on the small of my back to guide me through the bar, then kept it there as we headed down the street. I felt myself falling hard. This wasn't just a little spark of initial attraction anymore. The way he took control of me so casually made me ache and seemed to short-circuit thought completely.

"Tell me you're not a virgin," he murmured when a stoplight forced us to wait on a corner.

"I'm not."

He gave me a little look. "Tell me you've been fucked up the ass before."

I swallowed, wondering how such a small, dirty sentence could be so hot. "I have."

The light turned. "Good," Ben said, and led me through the crosswalk.

By the time we got to his apartment, I was completely crazy for him. He piloted me backward into the nearest wall and kissed me firmly, and I rashly grabbed for his package, squeezing it. He let out a moan of surprise and thrust into my hand, his hips executing tight rolls that forced me to think about what he'd be like inside me. "Please," I moaned, kissing him desperately.

"Please what?" he breathed, sliding a hand between my legs.

"Oh god," I choked, "please fuck me." I'd never said that to anyone in my life, but Ben seemed to demand it.

"That sounds so good coming from a nice clean boy like you," Ben growled in my ear, pinning me to the wall with a knee between my thighs. He still smelled like the kitchen—grease, garlic, and fish, not a combination I'd have found sexy until then.

"Please fuck me," I moaned again, emboldened by his praise, by the fact that this was a guy who'd been around, who wouldn't be offended by things I'd had to keep to myself back home.

Ben sank his teeth into my neck, forcing a yelp out of me. "Gonna fuck you hard," he muttered, dragging me further into his apartment. I followed, stumbling, so desperate for him that I pulled my shirt over my head as we went. Ben followed suit, dropping his jacket at the bedroom door and his T-shirt beside the bed. Before I could go any further, he grabbed the front of my belt and tugged downward. "I want that mouth on me."

I'd never been manhandled to my knees like that before, and

I was desperate to at least open my slacks and let my cock spring free. I wanted to please Ben, though, and I was willing to put up with the discomfort—especially once he shoved his jeans down to his ankles and kicked them aside. His cock jutted straight out at me, so hard that it had turned a vivid crimson. The head glistened with precome, and as I watched, it throbbed steadily. I almost wanted to laugh giddily—it was all for me.

"Suck it," Ben ordered.

I grabbed his hips and drew the sticky head into my mouth, moaning softly as I licked. Ben moaned, and the thought that I was pleasing him spurred me on to trot out every trick I knew. I slid one hand down to fondle his balls while I sucked, and they moved against my hand, drawing up tight. I had to pull back to breathe, so turned on that coordinating sucking and breathing was a little beyond me.

"Take off your pants," Ben said. I stumbled to my feet and shoved them down and off. I was harder than I could remember being in years, and Ben nodded approval, wrapping a hand around my cock.

"Oh—fuck, be careful," I blurted.

Ben raised an eyebrow.

"Gonna come," I explained, managing a sheepish grin.

"I'd better fuck you before that happens." He hesitated, though, still staring at me, and squeezed my cock.

"Oh, fuck," I moaned, rising up on my toes to press harder into his hand even though I knew one more good stroke would do me in. I wanted to get fucked more than anything, but convincing my body to wait when his hand was right there was nearly impossible.

"Get on the bed," Ben said, finally releasing my cock.

Glad that he'd made the decision for me, I sprawled out on his bed on my back, figuring that if he wanted me some other way, he'd make it known. From the nightstand, he pulled out a condom for himself and lube for me. I was nervous about preparing myself while he watched—what if I did it in some way he'd never seen before?—but the handing over of the Wet was a pretty obvious suggestion that I do just that. I slicked up my fingers, spread my legs, and tried to push two fingers in as I usually did. It hurt. Surprised, I tried one; that was better, but there was still something wrong.

"You're nervous," Ben said. He gestured for me to stop and lubed up his own fingers. I couldn't help feeling skeptical; if I was nervous with my fingers, I couldn't imagine being any more relaxed with Ben's.

He rested his hand on my abs and massaged gently, then massaged my hole to the same rhythm. Before I knew it, he had two fingers in, scissoring them gently. "Wow," I moaned.

"You're so fucking tight," Ben said. "It's going to hurt to fuck you."

I grinned, already flying a little on the exquisite sensation of his fingers inside me. "Hurt me or hurt you?"

"Maybe a little of both." He smiled back at me, then thrust sharply with his fingers. I gasped and immediately canted my hips up for more. He chuckled, pulling his fingers out and wiping them on a towel. "Seems like you're ready," he teased.

"God, yes, fuck me, please." I shoved a pillow under my hips and spread my legs wide.

Ben pulled on the condom and settled between my thighs, looking down at me quietly one more time.

"Fuck me," I whispered.

Something in his eyes changed, and he arched up to position himself, one hand wrapped around his cock. He was bigger than my other two lovers had been, and the nerves didn't help me open up, but he kept pressing and pulling back, pressing and pulling back, and soon when he pressed he slid inside. I moaned, grabbing the blanket beneath me, and he grabbed my hands and put them on his shoulders. "Leave marks," he said.

I managed a breathless laugh and hung on to him just as hard as I'd been gripping the blanket, my fingernails digging into his skin. He began to thrust, so slowly that I could feel how the head gave way to the shaft and back again. My cock lay tight against my abs, and every occasional brush of his belly against the underside was an exquisitely welcome torture.

His thrusts quickened, and when they grew sharp I cried out, stunned by how good he felt so deep inside me. I didn't have to try to leave marks anymore; my fingers were clawing around his shoulders without any conscious thought on my part. He fucked me so hard that I slid up the bed in tiny jerking motions, his breath short and hot in my face, his sweat burning where his hips rubbed against my thighs. Somewhere in the haze of sensation I began to beg, and when his rough, kitchen-calloused hand wrapped around my cock and squeezed I think I screamed. I felt my come spurt over my chest, heard Ben's startled grunt, and then he shoved me down hard into the bed, fucking me fast and hard as he came deep inside me.

Abruptly, it was quiet, just our heavy breaths filling the room. "Jesus," I moaned, resting one hand on Ben's overheated back.

"Yeah." Ben wiped his sweaty forehead on my chest, then looked up at me. He grinned, his hair every which way, his face red. "Welcome to the big city."

Scott was mock-furious that I didn't get the truffle torte recipe, but when Ben didn't return my calls, Scott quit playing and started buying me drinks. The weird thing is, I didn't mind. The sex had been amazing, and I would have liked more of it, but Ben gave me something else that was more important: he showed me that I could go get what I wanted. That was what moving to the city was all about: leaving behind the lockstep of small towns and pursuing my own thing, without fear that an entire community would turn against me. As great as the sex was, it wasn't quite as great as figuring that one out.

Thanks, Ben.

HOOKING UP

J. M. Snyder

We arrange to meet at Fairpark Mall because neither of us is ready to bring the other home just yet. It's been three weeks since we met, an eternity online, but I'm still cautious. I know what he says he looks like, know who he claims to be, but nowadays you never can tell.

I'm waiting outside the food court, leaning back against the wall with my hips thrust forward and the usual scowl on my face. My black clothes must look like a bruise against the white-washed bricks. Through my dyed bangs, I watch people avoid looking at me as they pass. Most grimace at my goth getup; a brave few laugh. Fuck them.

Damien's late.

For the hundredth time since I agreed to meet him in person, I wonder if that's his real name. I wonder what he'll call me. I go by *Broken* online, a shortened form of my username *brokenboy*, but in one email, I confessed that my parents named me Brandon and he hasn't called me anything else since. How stupid would it sound, asking him to call me by my login name when we're standing face-to-face? I shift my weight from one foot to the other and hope there won't be much talk between us once he finally shows up. We can talk online, through IMs or blog comments. I'm under the impression here that we're getting together for so much more.

Supposedly he drives a black car—I've seen pics of it on his page. But now that I'm looking for it, every car circling the mall seems to be black. What if he's just cruising the lot, checking me out? I run a self-conscious hand through my spiked hair and glare at the world around me in general. What if he's watching me right this minute? Or if he's already driven by, didn't like what he saw, and left me hanging? I'll go home and log online just to find some lame excuse in my in-box: *Sorry dude, something suddenly came up.* I pick at the hem of my tight black T-shirt, tug it down to meet the waistband of my black jeans, smooth it across my stomach and feel the heat of the morning sun where it's warmed the fabric.

I'm surprised to find how damn nervous I am. I've done this before, met guys online and scheduled to hook up with them in real life, but Damien's the first one I've really felt anything for, if I'm being honest. He's the first person I've ever connected with and it fucking *scares* me, the way he's managed to slip into my everyday existence in such a short span of time. If he bails on me today…if he doesn't even bother to *show*…

A familiar black Camaro turns at the light and zooms through the lot, heading straight for me. As it nears, I recognize the face behind the wheel as the one on Damien's webcam—so he really *is* hot as shit. Narrow jaw, chiseled cheekbones, dark eyes like ink pooled in the hollows of his face. Long black hair, dyed like mine I'm sure, wispy against his pale skin. When he sees me staring, he flashes a roguish grin that shakes my world and I swear the car lunges forward with a sudden burst of speed.

At the last possible second, Damien turns the wheel and eases to a stop at the curb in front of me. Then he cuts the engine and steps out before I can push away from the wall. With quick strides he comes at me, a commanding look in his eyes that makes my dick take notice. I'm just about to say something stupid like, "Hey Damien," when he steps up beside me and leans against my arm. The chill of air-conditioning lingers around him, making him seem impossibly cool on such a hot day, but when he touches my bare midriff with black-tipped fingers, my flesh burns beneath his. He's a few inches taller than me and glowers as if trying to tattoo me onto his brain. When I start to speak, he covers my lips with his in a silencing kiss.

For one breathless moment, his tongue enters me. I lean back against the warm brick, not caring who sees us here outside the mall, with his hand on my stomach, one finger tracing my navel, as he licks inside my mouth. He fills my senses and tastes like cherry lollipops, his scent a mixture of patchouli musk and the sweet sting of pot. He weakens me. I fumble at his waist, finding one of the belt loops on his black jeans, then rub my hand up under his black tank top and over taut skin to finger one erect nipple, hard as a nugget of gold in my palm. *In public!* my mind screams, thrilled. The hand on my stomach slips lower, sneaks beneath the waistline of my jeans, his thumb still circling my navel as he kisses me again and again. I sigh when he pulls away, and gasp each time he delves, hungrily, deeper into me.

Then he straightens, his hand now tugging on the zipper of my jeans as he stands back. I can't seem to catch my breath and I pray that he doesn't ruin this with some flippant remark like the ones he tends to make online, when he thinks I'm getting too serious about things. About *us*. "Brandon," he murmurs in a raspy, smoked-out voice that I feel in the back of my throat. There's a teasing glint in his eyes that makes me anxious. "You sexy thang."

I laugh, trying to break this tension, but it doesn't work and I have to avert my gaze from his. "Damien," I say, because I can't think of anything else. He's so damn *intense*. Somehow the webcam photos failed to capture that. We must look a fright, two goths like smudges on the bright day, standing so close together that there's no doubt about what we're both here to do. As if the bulge at my crotch wasn't a clue. I'm painfully aware of Damien's hand just inches above where I want him to be. "So you want to go somewhere else?" I ask.

"Get in the car," he says, and pulls me along after him by the zipper of my jeans.

The leather interior of his Camaro is also black. Damien holds the door for me and I sink into the passenger seat, lowering myself down, down, until I feel like I'm sitting on the sidewalk. I'll have to roll myself out when we stop. The door slams shut, and with a few wide strides Damien reaches his side of the car and falls in beside me. He catches me in another kiss while I'm buckling the seatbelt, and laughs as the engine roars to life. "What?" I shout over the sudden blast of music, half-smiling, ready to share the joke. But he shakes his head, shifts from first to third without hesitation, then zooms out of the parking lot. His hand strays from the gearshift to my thigh, and his fingers tap against my dick as he keeps time with the music. Each beat shudders through me. By the time we've cleared the mall, I'm hard.

We don't speak. Funny—we've said so much to each other online that we've saved nothing for when we finally meet. He keeps one hand on my thigh and shifts gears with the other, steering with his knee when necessary. Over the pounding music, he says my name. "What do you have in mind?" I ask. His hand eases into my lap to pluck at my zipper. I laugh, my stomach more than a little anxious at his touch. Did I say I've done this before? I lied.

"I know a place," he tells me, as if that's explanation enough. I don't ask how he knows or where it might be. Instead I watch his hand work in my lap, and after an eternity, I finally talk myself into placing mine over it. He turns his hand over, and his grip is warm and confident. I like the way his black nail polish looks, like little glossy squares where his nails are. His fingers curl around mine, holding me fast, and my dick strums with desire just a thin layer of clothing away.

Before I know it, we've pulled into the parking lot of a rundown motel that looks like it caters to truck drivers and prostitutes. From the way Damien drives past the office, I figure he must have stopped already and gotten the key before picking me up. We pull around behind the motel and coast to a stop at the end of a long row of rooms. Damien extracts his hand from mine and yanks up the parking brake. "We're here."

I clamber out of the Camaro, an exit much less graceful than Damien's. While I'm straightening my shirt, trying unsuccessfully to stretch it down enough to cover the obscene outline of my dick in the front of my jeans, Damien comes around the back of the car and hooks one of my belt loops on his way by. There's a black messenger bag slung over his back. "Props?" I ask as he leads me to the door of our room. His smile intrigues me. Suddenly I wonder if there was anything I should have brought, but other than the handful of condoms shoved into my back pocket, I can't think of what else we could possibly need. Lube maybe, but the condoms are heavily lubricated and I'm sure there's a free minibottle of lotion in the bathroom just waiting to be put to good use.

Inside, the room is sparsely furnished—one large bed, a night-stand with a phone, a huge mirror that dwarfs the small dresser beneath it, a lamp that's already on. "I see you've been here," I say as I close the door behind me.

Damien shrugs and the bag slips off his shoulder to the bed. "Once or twice," he admits.

I so didn't need to know that. "I meant—"

He gives me a saucy wink I've seen before, through the lens of his webcam. "I'm kidding," he says, but I don't quite believe him. With a pirouette, he flops onto the bed and leans back, checking me out.

I glance about the room, searching for something to focus on, something safe, something not Damien, but he's like a vortex in the center of my world. No matter where I look he's there, in the corner of my vision, watching me. Where's this nervousness coming from? This isn't me. Online I'm so much cockier, so different. Trying to keep that in mind, I ask, "Like what you see?"

"I can look at you online," he replies. He shakes his long hair behind him and says, "Come over here and let me touch you already."

"What's in the bag?" I want to know. He doesn't answer, just reaches out and snags the waistband of my jeans to reel me in. I laugh as he thumbs open my fly. "You're all about jerking me around, aren't you?"

My zipper parts beneath his insistent hand. "I can jerk you off," he offers, a slight smile toying with the edges of his mouth. He has a wide mouth, much larger in real life than I imagined it to be, with strong teeth that flash when he grins and a tongue that's pink and tempting. I want to kiss him again, feel that tongue against mine, and I surprise both of us by climbing onto the bed above him. His hand rubs at the front of my underwear as I push him back, my mouth seeking his, but he waits until he's against the bedspread with nowhere else to go before he gives in to me. It's a rough kiss, desperate. Damien rubs my erection through my briefs, sending shivers of pleasure shooting through me with each stroke, and I hump against him, my legs splayed on either side of his hips, my weight bearing down into the palm of his hand. Some very small part of me is aware of his other hand fumbling at the bag beside us, unzipping it blindly, reaching inside for whatever he's got in there, and for a brief second I wonder if he has a fetish I don't know about yet, if he's pulling out a huge dildo he plans to ram into me, or maybe whips and chains. But the reason we agreed to meet like this, the reason we even started *talking* online, is that he's a bottom and I'm not. He's been adamant about that from the start. Behind my closed eyes, I can see the line of text from his instant message: *when we hook up just remember i'm the one getting fucked brandon, alright? i'm dying to have that thick cock of yours shoved so far into me i can taste it in the back of my throat.* This, two days after I sent him a webcam shot of my dick, something I'd never done before, but look where it got us.

Damien works down the front of my briefs, exposing my cock and tucking the material below my balls. I break away from him long enough to get a look at whatever it is he's taken out of the bag, only to find myself blinded by the sudden flash of a camera. I push away from him and roll off, hurt. A *camera?* While we're—

"Damien!" I cry, scrambling to the edge of the bed. But I misjudge the distance, the pants around my hips don't give me much movement, and I fall to the floor in a horny, aching heap. My underwear bites into the tender skin below my balls and I struggle to pull it into place, but I'm too hard and too close to coming to be able to force myself back into the confines of those

briefs. A camera. To take pictures of what, us? Me? For who?
If he's posting this shit online... He rolls to the side of the bed,
looks down at me, that damn grin still in place. As I fight with
my clothing, I spit out, "Fuck you."

"Brandon," he starts. A gentle hand smoothes over the top
of my head but I shake it away. It settles on my shoulder and I
scoot out of reach. "Listen to me," Damien says, his voice low
and comforting. "Brandon, it's not what you think."

"I think you're fucking sick," I tell him. Somehow I get to
my feet, but my hard shaft points directly at Damien's face and
when he takes a playful bite at it, I turn my back to him. "What
are the pictures for, your blog? I'm not some show-off *cam* boy
like you."

"You sent me that pic of your dick," he points out.

"For your eyes only!" I tell him. I'm amazed that I'm still so
hard for him despite this. *Maybe because of it*, a voice inside me
whispers, but I refuse to believe that. "I thought we were here to
hook up," I tell him, finally pulling up my briefs. They're damp
and clammy against my skin, my hands smell of musk and sex,
my cock burns with a sweet fire that threatens to set me aflame
but I ignore it. I stagger as I try to pull my jeans up. "You never
said you wanted to document the deed."

Damien touches the small of my back. I'm precarious anyway,
teetering on one foot as I wrestle with the jeans, and it's all too
easy to fall back on the bed beside him. "Brandon," he murmurs,
kissing my shoulder. His lips are hot through my shirt. I want to
push him away again but can't. As if he knows this, he nuzzles
against me, forces his head under my arm to rub his nose into
my ribs. His hair feels impossibly soft beneath my hand. "My
little broken boy," he calls me, a play on my username that melts
whatever defenses I've tried to shore up between us. He says my
real name again, lays his head in my lap. My hand is on his back

now—when did he remove his shirt? He has two small wings tattooed between his shoulder blades, and I brush his long hair aside to trace the curve of the ink on his pale skin. He's playing with my dick again, one finger poking at the swollen head through my briefs. His breath tickles along my inner thighs. As if nothing happened, he asks, "You have any tats?"

I frown at the wings on his back. "No," I admit. I feel I have to add, "I've thought about it but haven't really decided what I want to get." Then, not ready to let him win yet, I ask, "What did you bring a camera for?"

He licks the front of my briefs and laughs. "I'm a cam whore, Brandon. You know that." When I don't reply, he says, "I wasn't going to put them online."

"What were you going to do with them?" I want to know.

He shrugs, a move that settles him on my lap, and his tongue licks out again, rubbing insistently at the slit in my cockhead. "Just get off on them later," he tells me. He kisses me through the briefs, his lips now working my hard length. "If you come now," he asks, "can you come again later when we fuck?"

"We're still arguing," I point out.

Damien grins against my crotch. "No, we're not."

I'm not so ready to give in. "Why didn't you tell me about the camera before?"

Another shrug—he's infuriating. "I didn't know the flash would go off."

"Damien!" I push him away but in one fluid movement, he slides off the bed and stands in front of me; unzips his jeans, hooks his thumbs into the waistband, pushes both jeans and underwear to the ground; steps out of the clothes, an uncut dick jutting from the swirl of black hair at his crotch, his eyes never leaving mine. He pins me in place with that stare like headlights in the night. I don't realize he's climbing onto me until he eases me to the bed, and then it's too late to hold him back. "Damien, no," I try, but my hands touch his flat stomach and find their own way up the narrow plane of his body, over the tattooed vine that trails from his navel to circle around one hard nipple, over his shoulders to cradle his jaw in my palms as I pull him in for another kiss. His lips glance off mine to suck at a sensitive spot behind my ear and I sigh into the sheet of his hair that tickles beneath my nose. "You're evil," I tell him.

He laughs, a little breathless, and says, "You like it." His hands rub along my sides, pushing my shirt up out of the way, and then he sits down on my throbbing crotch, pulls the shirt off over my head, and tosses it aside. He fingers the camera beside us on the bed. "Can I?" he asks.

I want to say no, but I don't want to lose what we have between us, this moment or the past three weeks or how he makes me feel, the surge I get whenever I see his name in my inbox, the strangling rush of lust when he looks my way. "Swear to me that the pictures don't go online."

His smile is promise enough. "You're so sexy," he tells me as he brings the camera to his face. I try not to feel self-conscious when the flash goes off, but I still feel exposed and vulnerable and not a little bit used. As if he knows this, Damien rocks above me, rubbing his ass against my still-hidden dick. "Smile for me," he says.

I do, but it's a halfhearted gesture. "Are you going to want to do that while we're getting it on?"

Damien makes a strangled sound and sticks his tongue out at me like a petulant little boy. "You're mean." He snaps off another picture or two, then tosses the camera onto the pillows beside us. "You're lucky I didn't bring the video feed. I could make a killing selling porno DVDs. Bel Ami has nothing on us." Before I can answer, he laughs. "I'm kidding. Don't you trust me?"

"I thought I did," I say.

"You do," he assures me. He starts to stroke himself, the head of his cock peeking out at me from the foreskin, and I have to touch it, just to see what it feels like in my hand. When I thumb over the knob, creamy juice trickles out. Damien takes my wrist and makes me lick it. He tastes salty and just a little bitter. When I reach for him again, eager for more, he catches my hand and laces our fingers together. "Where are the condoms?" he wants to know.

"My back pocket." I try to touch him with my other hand, but he grabs that one, too, then spreads my arms out to either side and leans down over me for a quick kiss. I whisper into him, "No fair."

"I don't know about you," he says, his words mere breath against my skin, "but I'm ready to get fucked. Roll over." Before I can comply, he rolls me onto my side and digs out a handful of condoms from the pocket of my jeans. They scatter beside me on the bed. Then Damien tugs on my jeans and briefs, pulling them down as he scoots to the edge of the bed. I kick off my shoes and pants and he crawls back on top of me. Then he presses against me, his hips rubbing our cocks together, his shaft as hard and unyielding as my own. For a brief moment we kiss, his arms encircling me, trapping me between him and the bed. Just as I begin to move against him, though, he sits up and straddles me again. "Cheers," he says as he rips open a condom packet. With expert moves, he rolls it onto my shaft and leans above me for another kiss. "Guide me into you," he whispers.

Holding the condom tight around the base of my dick, I massage my balls while my other hand rubs between Damien's legs in search of entry. I find his puckered hole and finger it, which makes him moan my name in a guttural voice. I ease him down, his hands fisting in the sheets on either side of my head, his mouth open, cheeks slack, brilliant eyes closed in pleasure.

When I'm inside, he sits on me, taking me in completely, and as he rocks against me, my hands push down against the tops of his thighs, holding him in place. We find a slow rhythm, steady; his muscles work at my cock, squeezing me to orgasm, and I thrust up into him over and over again as he moves above me.

At some point he opens his eyes, stares down into me, his gaze unwavering, consuming, devouring me. The intensity of his stare, the emotion I think I see behind his dark eyes, drives me to a shuddering climax and his name claws out of my throat in a hoarse cry with the force of my orgasm. Once I come, he scoots up closer, astride my chest, and lets me suck the tip of his dick while I work the foreskin back and forth, bringing him to release.

Later I agree to more pictures, if only because I like the way his eyes light up when he holds the camera in his hand. He takes shots of me sprawled on the bed, wrapped among the sheets, coyly peeking out at the lens. He likes my lips and wants close-ups of them on his dick, which I'm all too eager to taste again. Inside the bag are candles that he lights and places around the room. More photos, these of him dribbling hot wax onto my back, the curve of my buttocks. A shot of one lit candle precariously stuck a few inches into my ass—uncomfortable, yes, but I trust him and he says it looks incredibly hot, my hard cock sticking out between my legs at the same angle as the candle above.

Then it's my turn, and he wants me to take him from behind, camera clicking as I fuck him again and again, and I suspect he's converted me into a cam whore, too.

Because I'm tattoo-less, Damien uses a black marker to draw an intricate design that swirls from one hip bone to the other and spans the space between my navel and dick. He hovers above me, the narrow marker ticklish on my skin, his hair like feathers where it brushes along my thighs. I lie back and stare at the ceiling while he works, trying not to breathe, but every now and then a giggle escapes my lips, and I have to sit up to check on his progress. He looks so serious, frowning at the lines he's inking onto my skin. "This is permanent?" I ask him.

"It'll come off eventually," he replies, distracted. His face is just inches above my crotch, and my dick keeps trying to stand up beneath his chin. He holds it down with one hand, which only makes it more eager for his touch. At one point, it brushes his cheek and he kisses it, an absent gesture that makes me laugh. I think I love him. Has it really only been three weeks? It feels like forever. The marker dances across my stomach as he draws and my skin flutters at the touch. "Brandon," he warns.

In the same warning tone of voice, I say, "Damien." He gives me a cautionary look, which only makes me sputter with stifled laughter. Then, getting serious, I ask, "Can we do this again?"

He blows across my belly. "Soon as the ink dries."

"I don't mean now," I tell him. At the questioning look he gives me, I explain, "We can have sex again, I'm not saying that. But I meant can we do this whole thing all over again? Like next weekend, or something?" His stare unnerves me, I can't read behind it, I have no clue what he's thinking. What if this is it for him? What if we go back to an online relationship that slowly unravels until we drift apart? What if— "What do you think?" I want to know. "I mean, about hooking up again—"

A sly grin pulls at his mouth and lights up his eyes. "Next weekend sounds good to me," he says. Then, recapping the marker, he sits up on the bed and stretches his legs toward my head. I grab one of his feet, then thread my fingers through his toes. Lying on his side, he rubs at my balls and asks, "Ever done a sixty-nine?"

In response, I slide down to take his uncut length into my mouth again.

COCKFIGHTING

Keith Peck

He speaks slowly, the blond one does, his voice scratchy from ambient cigarette smoke, over the very bluesy, very up-tempo music the band plays outside on the patio. It's not overly noisy inside the bar here at Sadlack's, since most everyone is on the patio swaying with the beat. But it's loud enough to keep him from being overheard.

"I'm not bullshitting you, pussy. I can make a dude cum twice, just from pluggin' his hole. Hands free." He gazes across the *U*-shaped bar, through the windows that look down on the parking lot in front of the Buddha's Belly, the skater-*cum*-head shop next door. "You're lucky if the guy even feels your prong."

He shifts his jean-clad ass on the stool, taps a square-toed boot against the bar. A golden Vandyke rings his lips. A dark blue bandana keeps his face free of his hair, but a flaxen cascade pours down his back. He is Snake, an appellation now so old it has become his true name. To those who inquire about his name, Snake explains by thrusting into their surprised faces his thickly muscled forearms, tattooed with anacondas entwined and thrusting reptilian penises at each other. He likes to punctuate the gesture with a Gene Simmons tongue-waggle and a Hannibal Lecter hiss.

"I make you cum, bitch," snarls Skunk, sitting next to him and slowly consuming a beer. He always seems more surly and angry than he actually is. Skunk is not Snake's brother, though the two have faked it in cheap motels at the top of their lungs. Beautifully long like that of his rival, Skunk's hair is straighter than Snake's; it's also black as his pungent namesake. While Snake is tall and athletic and his skin is for the most part un-inked beyond his forearms, Skunk is tall and lithe and is in the process of covering every square inch of flesh with tattoos. His loose fatigue pants, tucked into his boots, ride low enough on his hips to show a few inches of tattooed skin between his T-shirt and the belt loops. On one bicep, an assortment of disembodied, red-veined eyes gazes upon an African-hued *jinni* emerging from a mighty bong.

"I can make any fucker cum, pussy," Skunk continues. "Tell you what. I'll let you watch me with that hot blond daddy. Last time his woman was out of town, he made like Texas and I made like the drilling rig, and Texas had three friggin' huge-ass gushers before the rig hit bottom." He sucks down his Miller. "You want another beer or you wanna go smoke that joint?"

"Beer," says Snake. "You're full of shit. I watched you with that guy, that Asian guy—"

"—Hey, that was a tight fucking ass! You had trouble that night with your fratbitchboy, too."

Snake, feigning great weariness, slowly shakes his head. "That was because that stupid fuck thought my cock was ripping him. I had to get rough to get it in. When I get rough, I quit looking to make my boy spunk."

"You get rough a lot," says Skunk. He signals the bartender, a voluptuous goth Valkyrie type with huge tits in a chain-mail bra.

"I got a big prick," says Snake.

"Mine's bigger."

"I make 'em scream."

"If they scream you're doing it wrong, pussy." Skunk flips five bucks to the Valkyrie. "They like it when they get it from me." He palms his groin. "I'm Trigger. I'm Mr. Fucking Ed. I'm the stallion and everyone's my mare and they always leave dripping my spooge and singing my fuckin' name."

But Snake doesn't reply. He has found prey.

He sees on the far side of the bar, where a narrow passage between the windows and the stools leads back to the toilets, someone he knows will help them. His name is Justin. A girl is talking to him. Justin is strong-shouldered and tight-waisted, almost like a Marine. His pectoral muscles strain, confined in a T-shirt very white against his obsidian skin. His hair is corn-rowed and enriched with red, yellow, and green beads. His lips are soft and dark and currently giving an absentminded but thorough blow job to a stiff and sweaty bottle of Budweiser. Those lips also like to nibble clitorises as well.

"Let's settle this," Snake says.

"This isn't ever going to be settled," says Skunk.

"That ain't the point, pussy." Snake inclines his head toward Justin.

Skunk glances across the bar and gets Snake's point. "Justin. Not sure if he'll go for it tonight. It's that time of the month, so he's been fucking that crazy girl from Cup-a-Joe's."

"Who doesn't?"

"You." Skunk regards Justin, notes the black guy's eyes flick toward his, hold his gaze. "Then again..."

"So you wanna?" asks Snake.

"Fuck yeah, cunt." Skunk stands, tugs his pants up because he's getting way too much air on his buttocks. He taps his shirt pocket, where two somnolent joints await their Prometheus. He moves off.

"Don't fuck it up!" Snake calls.

Skunk flips him the bird as he circles the bar. Justin, the girl next to him forgotten, sees the gesture and grins.

Skunk knows from the grin that Justin knows what's on his mind, and that Justin agrees, but the crazy girl from Cup-a-Joe complicates things, as does the girl next to Justin, who he has obviously decided he'd rather not fuck tonight. So Skunk pretends to knavery. "Hey, Justin. Wanna go smoke?" He rests a hand on Justin's shoulder. The warm flesh, familiar to both Snake and Skunk, does not shrink away.

Justin plays stupid. "Man, I told you, I don't smoke."

"This ain't tobacco," says Skunk *sotto voce*, in order to enhance the drama.

Justin's eyes glitter like emeralds in the sun. "That some of the—"

"Yeah. Come on. Snake wants to smoke too."

A few minutes later the three descend the stairs to the sidewalk, leaving a very pissed-off girl at the bar. Through a gap in the flow of traffic they dart across Hillsborough Street to the Belltower, and then cut down Pullen Road. It's a Friday, so the night pounds and palpitates with revelers, but the center of the frenzy is over on Western Boulevard and the swathe of park and university muffles the thunder. Girls are cruising by in Daddy's BMW, however, and all the drunk and most of the sober ones wolf-whistle the two rough-clad headbangers and the black muscled idol as they pass.

"We need some help," says Snake to Justin, who is grinning and waving sheepishly at some drunk high school bimbo hanging from a Mercedes convertible, inviting him to test the state's age of consent laws.

"Yeah?" As he turns away from the street, a ghostly smile plays on Justin's lips.

"We got a score to settle."

"Last Wednesday not settle it?"

"Nah."

"Figured. How much weed you got?" asks Justin.

"Lots," Skunk lies.

"I'm your bitch," says Justin. He peels off his shirt. Justin goes in a big way for kung fu and kendo. His torso has responded well. He is sleekly muscled, not overpowering. He exudes a dark, oily scent.

"Told ya," Skunk grins at Snake.

"Told me what, pussy?" says Snake.

Turning left into Pullen Park, they skirt the baseball field and descend into a tree-shaded railroad cutting. The night is silenced. This place is about as private as one can get here, in the middle of the city, though from time to time some of Raleigh's most assiduous alcoholics take up residence, usually when the get-tough politicians need reelection and run them off the streets.

Marijuana smoke blooms in the air like phantasmal cauli-flowers. The joint's orange tip reflects in Skunk's eyes. He sucks in a lungful, passes it to Justin. Justin tokes and passes to Snake. In silence they smoke, though all is not quiet in their crotches and nothing in their minds.

By the time the second joint has burned down to a roach, Justin has become unglued from his world and is adrift on a chiaroscuro plain lit by the stroboscopic flashing of the stars. The conversation has an unreal aspect, as if they are not true people who are speaking, but actors—puppets, really—uttering someone else's lines.

Out of it.

Toasted like a marshmallow.

Fucked that crazy chick? Really?

Laughter. *It was hot. I watched them. She like what he's got.*

Not as much as he likes what I got.

Fuck you, cunt, I'm going first.

Stand back, pussy, and I'll show you how to fuck.

A disembodied hand touches Justin's face. Another touches his butt. Justin sees Skunk's torso, naked and sinewy. And Skunk's crotch, enticingly tented. Snake's hot, beer-scented breath caresses his neck. Relaxing, he laughs.

Skunk observes the redness in Justin's eyes, the slack shoulders, the stiff nipples like hard kernels of popcorn. He grins at Snake, whose blond waves loom over Justin's shoulder like a sunrise. "Ready?"

"Fuck yeah," says Snake. His eyes narrow to faintly yellowish slits. "Now I'm going to show you how to breed a man right."

He encircles Justin's waist from behind, pulling the hard-muscled body against his. His fingers dig into the man's shorts.

"Not commando tonight?" asks Snake.

"No," Justin sighs, leaning his head back against Snake. Snake's lips nuzzle his ear. His fingertips find the thick waistband of Justin's jockstrap, slip into the steamy pouch.

"You smell good," says Snake.

"Blame your buddy." Justin has acquired Skunk's distaste for deodorant, and he is darkly pungent, powerful, like the smell of a canvas coffee sack.

"He ain't evil enough to be my buddy," croons Snake. His hand slips beside Justin's prong, cups the black boy's heavy nut sac, judges the load of cream.

"*He's* my bitch," says Skunk. He shimmies out of his fatigues. Naked save for the glorious ink. The word *satyr* arches over his navel, in elaborate Gothic capitals. Faces demonic and boyish and manly and equine leer from his thighs. A soft trail of hair, dense but downy, descends from his navel to his groin, thickening to dark whorls rank with scent. A wrinkled foreskin like an elephant's hide hoods his fat, blunt cockhead. Flecks of old, dry smegma crust the exposed edge of his foreskin, partially retracted over the oily, reeking cockhead. His balls swing in a loose sac between his knees, dangerously swollen. He smells like a bin of sweaty Judas Priest concert T-shirts.

"Make yourself useful," Snake says. "Strip the bitch."

Skunk undoes Justin's fly, and his khaki shorts fall bunched around his feet. The jock pouch is distorted by Justin's titanic meat, freakish even by porn standards. "All yours, bitch."

Snake kneels. Skunk's fingers roam down the strap clinging to the right buttcheek, and find that fragrant nexus between a man's legs where asshole and buttcheeks and nut sac and thighs converge. He finds a thick and greasy substance that slimes his fingers. Snake takes a whiff, then thrusts his fingers at Skunk. "Smell that, man? That's cunt. That's a woman's cunt you're smelling. This boy's been breedin'."

"We all got our kinks," Justin grunts.

Snake crushes Justin's left nipple between his fingertips. He convulses, as if a defibrillator were shocking him, a modern Lazarus.

"Awesome," says Skunk. He leans forward, inhales the funk rising from the yellowed, straining pouch. "Fucking awesome."

"Sweet boy," Snake croons into Justin's ear. He opens his fly, exposing his long dong, a fat cudgel with a brutally blunt head. His balls cling to the underside of the shaft like two tightly packed lemons. He bends and thrusts his face between Justin's buttocks.

"Christ," Justin mutters. He loves it. He loves how it feels to have a man lapping at him *there*, like a dog. Girls won't do that, no matter how much be begs, how long he spends satisfying them, how often he laps at them, no matter how many times he makes them cum.

Lured by Justin's potent reek, Snake burrows into the buttcrack. Justin did shower last night, but he's been vigorous since then—a ten-mile predawn run with the campus ROTC; a postclass workout, hard and long; fucking Audrey long and hard late in the afternoon. Justin's aroma is a garden of dangerous herbs and sharp spices.

Snake's tongue laves the ass crevice. Slimy buttflesh slithers over his face, raw and sour. Pulling back, his nostrils still thick with Justin's scent, he peels apart the muscular buttocks with his thumbs. A chocolate pucker nestles inside, clenched tight, not a fortress of virtue but an experienced cavern of delight. Snorting and puffing like a stallion, Snake's tongue charges for that doughnut, puckering and simpering at him like a braindead whore.

Playfully, Justin puckers his hole tight as a Baptist needing to shit during the pastor's peroration. Snake's tongue dances minuets on the hard ring. Tightly curled hair abrades his chin. He is frustrated. He wants to penetrate, not lick.

"Come on," Snake croons, "open up." He reaches forward into the jockstrap, takes Justin's nuts again, and slowly begins to stroke them. Justin cries out and his eyes roll up. Snake's tongue administers a delightful Templar kiss between strong Saracen buttocks. Justin yields to the serpent, grunting as the tongue slips into him.

The raw tang of jockbutt doesn't satisfy. It makes Snake want more. He wants to breed. He frees himself with a slurp from the spit-soaked pucker, stands.

"Ain't he a good kisser?" Skunk pulls a small bottle of lube from his fatigues and tosses it to Snake.

Justin pants like a dog, too far lost in his anticipatory moment.

"Thanks, pussy," says Snake. He smears lube on his cock, leans into the sweaty, glistening flesh. As he lines up his cock, he teases himself with Justin's wet, sloppy asscrack. Snake likes the thrill he feels shooting between his nuts and his cockhead. It inspires him to fuck like a god.

Skunk's gaze is level and serious. "Do it."

The wisdom of this situation requires that Snake, for once, obey his buddy. The blunt pink head rips open the prim flesh circle. Justin bucks; a low moan oozes from him as the gigantic shaft splits him. His hole, like Eve's, must stretch to take the Serpent.

"Oh yeah," Snake purrs. He grins, and begins to show off, just like they used to on the playgrounds. He has known his buddy since they were children. Giving the braided and willing bitch no time to adjust, he thrusts his cock ruthlessly inward, exploiting that soft opening in the hard flesh. Justin squeaks like a rat as Snake sheathes himself fully in mancunt. Justin's ravaged flesh convulses in a futile effort to disgorge Snake. Snake revels in Justin's defeat, his balls throbbing against Justin's squirming nut sac.

Skunk, fisting his shivering flesh, salutes his buddy's show. His foreskin moves with soft slurps over his cheesy head, and a strand of precum sways like a strand of spider silk in the night's uncertain air.

Justin shuts his eyes. These guys are good. This is why he gives himself to them when they ask. He bends forward, rests his forearms on his thighs just above his knees, riding the celestial agony of a dragon cock jammed deep into his bowels.

Snake surrenders to the need to thrust. But the simple in and out wouldn't have been showing off. He interweaves intricate themes into the simple thrusts of his fucking—corkscrews, twists, off-axis thrusts, subtle rotations of his meaty shaft. An artist of the flesh, his leaking cockhead paints Justin's rectum with his spicy precum. Madness tinges Justin's moaning as his cunt absorbs with soft squelches the headbanger's fat prong. Snake looks over at Skunk, grins triumphantly.

Suddenly, in the midst of the show, Snake feels Justin's butthole clenching, a gratifying flurry of constrictions on his prong. Snake recognizes the rhythm, because he's used to feeling that twice-a-second pulse of a prostate explosively depressurizing. He just didn't expect to bring off a recently laid Justin so easily. He grins, slips a hand into the jock pouch, pulls out fingers dripping with gray goo. He shoves his fingers under Skunk's face.

"That's one!" he chortles.

Justin's semen on Snake's fingers remind Skunk how his old Jockeys used to smell back in junior high, after he woke from a night of frenzied dreams.

Snake slams Justin's hole a few more times and then pulls out, his shaft still erect. A serious fight between himself and Skunk, this is not some simple exercise in nut-busting. Justin's cunt emits a profuse string of soft, moist farts. Rivulets of mucus ooze down Snake's cockshaft. Snake's soaked pubic thatch smells of butt and jism.

Skunk smacks palms with Snake. Now tagged, his nude body the dark core of his distinctive aroma, he takes the black boy's hips in his hands and positions him for breeding. He cannot help himself; he begins to gnaw one of Justin's braids.

"No romance," Snake barks. "Fuck the bitch."

"Yeah," groans Justin. "No goddam romance."

Skunk coughs up a thick gob of spit, smears it onto his shaft.

Spit and headcheese foam into gooey, smelly mess as he jerks his meat.

"Now," he breathes into Justin's ear, "here's the best fuck you're ever gonna have. *Bitch.*"

Tugging his foreskin back, he smears the rancid, almost liquid cheese on Justin's ring. His cockhead makes one circuit of the butthole before he thrusts. Justin's whorish groan—like a guitar chord, heavily distorted, guttural, passionate, full of yearning—echoes dangerously over the park as he plays the slut with gusto.

Skunk's thrusting starts slowly, he restrains himself from reaching a swift crescendo. Justin's rectum is a cunt best savored with a measured pace. The long shaft saws away at his butt and each of the rutting bucks indulges in the heat and warmth of the other. Justin, appreciating a stud-gourmand like Skunk, responds in the incoherent manner that is the highest and most civilized mental state he can currently attain: his groans slowly dissolve into gurgles, and then trail away.

"Watch, pussy," Skunk snarls at Snake. "Watch me fuck this guy. Watch and learn."

"Eat shit, Darth Pussy."

The motion of Skunk's hips becomes erratic, even chaotic. His balls describe loops in phase-space around the strange attractor of Justin's asshole. As Justin accepts Skunk's cock, an infinite, blissful realm seeps into his soul. He rides it for as long as he can, but he's not able to resist these guys for long. Within thirty seconds his gasps are rapid-paced, explosive. His anus quivers, anticipating orgasm.

But quickies aren't Skunk's style. He rips his cock outward until his fat cockhead lodges in Justin's anus like a cherry pit. He feels the ecstasy drain from Justin's flesh in the same way an evening rain in July kills the fireworks show. In his cruel denial, he exposes Justin to a different notion of sexual divinity. Then he indulges his cruelty further: his hand slaps in actinic bursts of pain on Justin's ass.

Snake is contemptuous. "You ain't doing it for him. You remember last time?"

"Shut up, pussy." Skunk doesn't care if Snake's too stupid to appreciate his tactics. He spears Justin deep, unleashes a flurry of thrusts, fucking like a rabbit on speed. Raw rectal tissue, swollen and wet, glides over his stone-hard cock. He opens Justin's asscheeks, staring at the purpled flesh his cock violates. Lube and mucus glisten on his ramrod.

The black boy likes to be held down. And used. Fucked. Bred. He's the pupil, Skunk the teacher; the subject: studding. Justin surrenders to Skunk's lesson, choking and groaning and spitting as his huge dong unleashes another potent flood into his dripping jockstrap.

Triumphantly, Skunk rips free. "That's one apiece, fuck-head," he says to Snake. He grips his cock at the base, brandishes it like a sword.

"Took you long enough."

Justin, with creaking muscles, rises from his crouch. Thick sperm clots his jockstrap.

"You're going nowhere," Snake says.

"You aren't kidding," says Justin. He finds a patch of soft pine needles, lies down, lifts his legs.

"All right," says Snake. He kneels, spreads Justin's dark strong thighs. His cock finds the hole again, and he sheathes himself in it like Excalibur in stone. "Bitch," Snake laughs. "You're loose as a cow." He begins pumping hard.

"I got the bull cock," says Skunk.

"Horse cock, dumbfuck," snaps Snake. He's rapidly approaching the point where he needs to juice. His balls hum like a power generator. But there's a war on, so he fights the urge. He's got to make Justin spunk again.

Snake glides his fingertips over Justin's sweat-streaked muscular flanks. There is no hair on the polished obsidian skin, not even the hard nipples. Snake strokes the nipples as if he were the breeze, even as he pounds furiously into the wet and sloshy cavern of Justin's asshole. Justin responds to the ecstasy, melting beneath Snake's pounding fury. Encouraged, Snake crushes the nipples, stretches them into long tentacles of pain. Justin's soft moans become squeals and screams that threaten to shatter him. Snake joins his noise-making, though with the objective of escaping orgasm, not achieving it.

By a few seconds, he does escape.

Justin twitches and spasms, then looses a weak volley of sperm into his jock like a breeding stallion near the end of an active day.

"There," gasps Snake, ripping out of the hole. "Two. I fucking told you. I make my bitches cum twice." His balls boil, desperate to breed. "Shit." He pinches his cockhead.

"Shit is right," says Skunk. "He barely felt that."

Justin's exhausted panting contradicts him, but that's not the point, and everyone knows that.

Skunk mounts up and thrusts home. Justin's rectum, once tight as a glove, is loose, floppy, and wet as a mare's pussy. This is to Skunk's advantage, and he knows it. Though the succulent flesh tempts him, he resists the urge to take the long plunge, to stroke those guts deep with the mindless intent not of showing off for Snake but purely, selfishly relieving the crippling pressure in his own balls. An experienced warrior accustomed to battle-grounds inside a young guy's butt, he fights off the urge.

Still, it's been a long night. He's drenched with sweat. And his nuts *hurt*. So he slips his thumb inside, curls it, jabs Justin's prostate. An old standard, and it's almost cheating, but both of them have used the tactic before. And it's successful. Justin cums, a thin watery discharge not unlike dog saliva. Gasping desperately, Skunk rolls off, his cock throbbing.

"You suck," snorts Snake. Contemplating how he's going to empty them, he idly strokes his nuts.

"That's two apiece," Skunk pants. "Fuck this crap. Let's get a nut."

Snake laughs. "Now you're talking."

His face dripping, Justin's eyes alight on the twin prongs. He knows what the headbangers are thinking. "I'm gonna be sore."

"But happy," says Skunk.

They shift positions without speaking, because they know what needs to be done. Skunk reclines on the pine needles, his dong thrusting skyward. Justin squats over him and stuffs the headbanger's huge cockhead into his churning cunt. Skunk moans, feeling his meat invading Justin. His pubic hair crushes against the tight buttcrack. Snake, kneeling behind Justin, rests a hand between the black boy's shoulder blades and bends him forward. Moving his cockhead down the sweaty, gooey furrow, he finds his buddy's iron-hard shaft. The sloppy ass ring laves his cockhead with transparent slime. Using Skunk's shaft as his guide, he begins to work his way inward.

"You fuckers are gonna kill me." Justin relaxes, his eyes rolling up, his shoulders sagging not in defeat but in anticipation of a sublime victory. Snake's fat prong elicits a sharp cry as it plunges suddenly into the hot cavern. Justin's exhausted thighs tremble.

Skunk, feeling his buddy's entry, bucks hard, ramming his belly against Justin's nuts. He duels Snake's meat, feeling their urethras pulse against each other. Justin's rectum flexes on their shafts, crossing them like sabers.

"Oh, that's it," Skunk says. Because now he feels Snake's nuts against his, and he'd kill for that feeling of his buddy's potency united with his own.

"Yeah, man," Snake says hoarsely.

"Shut up, you fucking morons," Justin hisses, "and screw me."

Helpless before the awesome urge swelling their balls, they begin to work.

Fighting an incredible ejective pressure, Snake drives full-length thrusts slowly up the hot black boy's velvet cunt. A pungent, sweaty sheen adorns the swaying sac of his nuts. He takes full responsibility for the thrusting, for Skunk can only move slightly. He grins, knowing that their orgasms will be his responsibility. His buddy and the bitch will both cum when Snake wills it.

Feeling like a parachutist does in those long, exquisite seconds before the chute opens, Skunk savors the debauchery of raw, tightly-packed flesh moving on his prong. Snake's cock, hard as concrete, thrusts eagerly alongside his own, and Justin's stretched anal hole fits his cock as if tailor-made. Their duet plays delightfully along his cock, notes as tightly coupled as their breeding bodies.

Eyes closed, his thighs burning from the effort, Justin rises up. His mouth is arid from the weed. He lives for this feeling—to be a cunt for a stud cock. Though he prefers pussy to cock, he's never disdained pleasure when offered. And this pleasure, to be a bitch to two studs who know what studding is, has benefited Justin many times in the sack.

Justin opens his knees, presenting his butt like a mare should to her stallion. He wishes now he could scream, that he could attract attention, that some girl—like the one back at

Sadlack's—would come by and see him, here like this, fucked by two donkey-donged perverts. Because he wants people to see the depths of depravity he loves.

Balls about to burst, Snake plunges a dry finger into Skunk's tight butthole.

"Motherfucker!" snarls Skunk. The nova, incipient in his ball sac, erupts into Justin's night-shrouded bowels, and chars Justin's rectum at least ten feet up the tube of twisting flesh. The howls from his release penetrate the dreams of the somnolent houses and dormitories surrounding the park.

Snake, an evil treacherous bastard the equal of Brutus, Cassius, and Judas, just laughs. "Bitch."

Skunk's a stud, a breeder; the load is copious, something you'd see gushing from the sluices of Hoover Dam. The white goo clots on the thrusting cocks.

"About fuckin' time," grunts Snake. His eyes go blank, he whimpers, his gusher pours into Skunk's sea of sperm. Their cocks thrash like dinosaurs in conflict.

Justin, his ululations deathlike, unloads the dregs of his cream into the spunk-crusted jockstrap. No pounding for Audrey tonight. But the sperm that really matters is percolating in his cunt like some savage potion. She'll thank him tomorrow. He stands upright. With his legs parted and his buttocks open, the semen clotting his anus glistens like snot on black velvet.

Skunk and Snake's cocks slacken into long fleshy arcs rooted in their sweaty groins.

"That last nut," says Snake, "was mine."

"Bullshit," snaps Skunk.

"Tell him, Justin," says Snake.

"It was his," says Justin.

"You're full of shit," says Skunk.

"I'm full of cum." He farts, wetly, and a few teaspoons of

creamy spunk splatter on the ground. He sighs, glad for the relief. "Don't get pissed off, man," Justin says. He moves toward his shorts. "You got me last time."

"This ain't the end of this," says Skunk. "There's a party this Friday. Over at a fraternity in Chapel Hill."

"You talking about a rematch?" Snake laughs.

"You up for it?"

Snake grabs his thick meat, brandishes it at Skunk as if it were a red cape and his buddy a bull. "I'm up for it."

DUFFLE

Dallas Angguish

Ventura, California

Joey Verona celebrates his eighteenth birthday just before he leaves for college. His dad lets him have his first official beer. Just the one. He screws up his face and pretends it's the first time the amber liquid has touched his lips. He doesn't mention the sleepover at Leonard Spinkle's house when he and Leonard stole a six-pack from Mr. Spinkle's basement fridge and got drunk looking at a brutally soiled copy of *Playboy*.

Joey doesn't tell them about the crazed look in Leonard's eyes when he folded out Miss June, her yellow bikini cast aside like the plucked petals of a juicy flower. He especially doesn't tell them that, despite the inebriation, Miss June hadn't had the same effect on him as she had on Leonard, whose tongue became unhinged and hung fatly and hotly from his lips, a heat-swollen sausage, small droplets of drool forming at its end as Leonard's fingers danced feverishly over Miss June's stapled crease.

Joey had been more interested in the beach on which Miss June floundered like a nympho seal. The golden sand, the white-tipped surf rolling behind her left shoulder: perfect beach break. *Is that Malibu?* he wondered. *The surf's supposed to be really good there.* When he sobered up, his lack of interest in Miss June's crease caused him some anxiety but, after all, Malibu *is* Malibu.

His brother mails a present. A T-shirt from UCSC, where he's a grad student. Usually his brother Dean is a total fucker but the T-shirt's cool. It has a slug on the front, same one Travolta wore in *Pulp Fiction*. He gets from his parents a new white-collared shirt that he'll never wear and a Christian rock CD that his folks think is cool. The band is called *Deliverance*. Joey is sure the homoerotic subtext is not intended. The fact that he knows about the homoerotic subtext of *Deliverance* at all causes him some anxiety as well. He hates his senior English teacher for it. Mr. Purse was always showing them movies featuring this sort of thing. That's probably why the PTA had him sacked. Too much subtext.

Joey plays the CD once. Just for the laugh. His folks are sitting uncomfortably by the stereo, their rocker-recliners as still as stones. Cups of grape cola fizz noisily in hands rested politely in their laps. Their ankles are religiously crossed. After a few minutes his mom asks, "Does this rock, honey?" Joey suppresses a chuckle and tells her yes, it rocks.

That night he calls Zara and tells her he thinks they should break it off. He tells her there is no need to be sad about it. With him leaving for college, and her starting work as a manicurist, there will be plentiful new opportunities for both of them. They've only been together a few weeks so he doesn't expect the flood of tears and expletives that come his way.

"Plentiful new opportunities! Who the hell do you think you are, Joey Verona, the fucking voice of God?!"

She's always been dramatic. That's what drew him to her in the first place, that and the fact that she was amenable to intercourse. But now, with her threats to tell his parents that he'd popped her cherry on the old lawn chair in Leonard's basement, he wishes he'd gone for a more sedate kind of girl. Someone with no interest in fingernail art.

After kissing his mom and pop good-bye, he drives to Leonard's house to pick up his board. He's in the closet about *that* so he hides his board in Leonard's basement, where memories of beer and soft porn lurk like a freshly dumped girlfriend. He's been hiding that he surfs for years. His mother thinks he and Leonard are study buddies. She doesn't know that Leonard is next to a certified cretin. The only thing he studies is mega-titty porn.

Leonard is going to community college nearby to learn to be an accountant. He can't tear himself away from that basement, smeared as it is with his man-scent and discarded DNA. Joey is going to college up north, University of California Santa Cruz. The same college as his brother, and Dusty.

Dusty, short for Dustin Gray, is his brother's best friend. Joey was eight when they met. Dusty was twelve. For years Joey followed his brother and Dusty everywhere they went. Idolized them. Dusty was cool about it, always threw Joey a bone, a smile, a mussing of his hair, but Dean made his life hell, never wanted him around. It was Dusty who taught Joey how to surf when Dean couldn't be bothered. It was Dusty who gave him all his hand-me-down surf gear. It was also Dusty who said, just before leaving with Dean for college, "Sometimes Dean can be a prick. Don't let it bother you. You're a good kid."

For Joey, Santa Cruz won't be just a new town, new surf, or

new opportunities. It's where he can be his own man, choose his own friends and, no matter what Dean thinks, hang out with whomever he wants, including Dusty. He's been aching to leave all year. Ventura has been closing in on him. Every time he surfed he felt alone, tense, waiting for the future to come in with the next wave. More and more, as the summer passed, he'd been feeling like a kid crushed on the beach when his sand-tunnel caves in, unable to breathe, unable to stretch out or move.

He picks up his board without saying good-bye to Leonard, who is asleep in his bedroom upstairs. He casts a fleeting glance at the chair in the corner, its white and orange plastic glinting in the half-light of the basement, and heads out of there, back to his car, to escape. He turns onto the highway with a rush of excitement.

He's a free man. No more living under parental scrutiny. No more church, no more curfews, no more rules. No more having to jack off in the car because his mother is a sniffer-dog where semen is concerned. If it gets on his sheets or underwear she'll find it. Even the smallest drop. She checks the level of the shampoo and conditioner as well. She knows how much it takes to wash the family's heads of hair. Too little in the bottle means he'll get a nervous knock on his door and will have to endure her disappointed *my son's a sinner* look. So he's taken to parking out back of Wal-Mart and, armed with a Jack Johnson CD and some cooking oil from Leonard's mother's kitchen, driving himself to the edge and back again, depending on how busy it is at Wal-Mart, maybe a half-dozen times, before he blows into a paper towel (also from Leonard's mother's kitchen) and falls asleep with his pants down around his ankles. Thank the lord for tinted windows.

Willow Creek, California
Joey plans to stop halfway at Morro Bay, where on vacation as

boys he and Dean had thrown fish to yelping seals. It was fun
until Dean tried to force-feed him a rank pilchard, its white fishy
eyes looking at him with smelly disapproval. He thinks of Miss
June. Not wanting to ruin his day with that recurring anxiety,
but also because he's still pumped about his new freedom, he
heads straight through Morro Bay. He doesn't stop until he hits
Big Sur.

He's been meaning to check out Willow Creek, supposedly
the best wave on the central coast. He pulls into Willow Creek
picnic ground and is out of the car before the last spit of exhaust
leaves the tailpipe. He jogs to a spot where he can see both north
and south, checks the conditions. There's not much going on. A
few diehard locals are out, waiting patiently for a wave. Desper-
ation can sometimes send you out in anything.

He sucks in the salty air, zips up his windbreaker against the
chill and opens his senses to the sea, the vast sky, the sun spar-
kling on the water, the jagged rocks. Relaxes into the vibe. Overhead, clouds are moving in from the west, heavy clouds riding
on a cold wind. This means rain. Before long it starts to sprinkle.
Joey heads back to his car and settles down to eat the sandwich
his mother packed him, ham and cheese. Good stuff.

As he shoves the last morsel of sandwich into his mouth the
rain starts to really pelt down. It thunders on the roof of the
car. At first he thinks it might be hail but then he realizes it's
just raindrops the size of marbles, heavy as stones and falling at
high velocity. He feels as if he's in a cave behind a waterfall—the
downpour so thick he can't see more than a few feet from the
car. He watches. He listens.

Two surfers emerge from the veil of water, their boards
under their arms. They stop by a cherry red Ford Bronco parked
nearby. One of them, a lean guy with a typical surfer's blond
mop, his body encased in a glistening black wetsuit, puts down

his board while the other one, a stocky guy wearing Hawaiian boardshorts with a shaved head and tribal tattoos on his biceps, shelters his buddy and himself with his own board. The blond one retrieves keys from behind the front tire, unaware that they are being watched, opens the door and rummages for a towel.

This is a scene Joey has seen many times. Dusty had sheltered him in the same way during a thunderstorm last summer, had held off the rain while Joey peeled off his boardshorts and wrapped himself in a warm towel. It's what good buddies do.

The stocky guy's body shows muscle built from paddling in big surf. He has that sharply accentuated *V* that runs from his hips down to his groin. He says something to his friend and laughs. His friend, wetsuit now peeled down to his waist— nipples erect from the cold and lower ribs red from where they rubbed against the board—roughly dries his friend's cropped hair. When he pulls away the towel they remain standing close to each other. Joey thinks this is to avoid getting wet. Then they do something that surprises him deeply. The blond one leans in and kisses his buddy square on the lips.

The kiss goes on for what Joey thinks is a very long time. Their mouths move in unison in a way that means they have done this many times before. This is no awkward stolen kiss. The blond's hands stroke his friend's chest; the stocky man responds by maneuvering him up against the side of the Bronco, pressing his muscled torso against his blond friend, angling himself so that they are pelvis to pelvis.

Joey can't believe his eyes. For a minute his brain, unable to compute what he's seeing, makes him think he's seeing a guy dry humping a *thin blonde girl*, her fair hair splayed across the red hood. When he looks again he sees what's really there. Two guys grinding against each other on a Ford Bronco. The surfboard tips over a little and the rain begins to strike them. They stop,

smile at each other, and return to the business of getting dry.
Joey's mind freezes. He doesn't know what to think. *Surfers just don't do this kind of shit.* At least not the surfers he knows. Maybe these Big Sur surfers are made differently? The thing that gets Joey more is that the two don't look like they'd be into other guys at all. No evident fag gene. Neither one looks anything like Mr. Purse. Joey's shocked. Thrown. His heart is pounding. Then, after a couple of minutes, he laughs. He doesn't know why. He just laughs. He waits for them to pull out of the parking lot before he does the same. He doesn't want them knowing he saw them.

He gets a speeding ticket just outside of Santa Cruz. He's sweet as pie to the cop. Something has ticked over inside him. All the way from Big Sur to his new hometown he thought about the two surfers, over and over. What he came to was this: why the hell shouldn't those guys kiss? Why shouldn't they get a bit of heat wherever they can? No one's so rich with affection they should be picky where they get it. Who's he to begrudge a couple of boys a slow grind up against a cherry red Bronco? Hell, life isn't worth much without your buddies. And then, to his own surprise, he thinks about Dusty. He thinks hard about Dusty.

Santa Cruz, California
Joey has long admired Dusty, looked up to him, wanted to be exactly like him. No one else had ever let Joey be himself. No one else gave him the time of day. At times the four-year difference in age seemed an eternity, like when Dusty got his driver's permit, or reached drinking age. These landmarks for Dusty made Joey feel he was being left behind. Yet, other times, he and Dusty couldn't be closer. Like the time, after he'd been dumped savagely by a bitch of a wave and pushed onto slimy bottom rocks that cut his thigh open, Dusty held a towel to

his wound until it stopped bleeding, gently rubbing his shoulder all the while for reassurance. Or the time, after the disastrous encounter with Miss June and her paper crease, that Joey had snuck home to find Dusty asleep on the couch, his bare chest rising rhythmically in sync, it seemed, with the breeze from the open window. After Joey wakened him by tripping over some unknown obstacle, they had talked side by side in the dark for hours, about surf mostly but, in a quiet moment, when Dusty had looked into Joey's eyes, something stirred within Joey. He'd thought it was what they called brotherly love. Even though they weren't brothers.

But after the sight of two surfer boys kissing at Willow Creek, Joey wonders what might have happened if they hadn't heard his mother come into the hall on the way to the bathroom. Might that quiet, warm moment have turned into something else? Something like the moment those surfers shared under their board in the rain? If it had, he might not have minded. But only because it was Dusty.

That kind of thinking, Joey soon discovers, led to unwanted hard-ons from hell. Hard-ons he hates because they make him feel dirty and ashamed. His dreams are haunted by a visual: Dusty, eyes half-lidded, voice heavy with moans, broad chest glistening with sweat, arching his back as he cums. By day, Joey's boner twitches in his jeans, and he laughs, and tries not to think about Dusty, and then thinks he might cry. For the week after arriving on campus for the start of his school year, even though Joey's dreams exceed the intensity of his waking thoughts, dreams that empty his balls every night, he doesn't seek Dusty out. But he feels obsessed. Obsessed in the clinical sense. Not just a turn of phrase. He is freaked out. Frightened by the possibility...

When Dusty finally phones, fishing for an invite, Joey lies to prevent him from coming to his dorm room. In the end, sounding disappointed, not knowing why Joey is being so cold, Dusty turns the conversation to Dean. "Dean and I don't see each other much these days," he says, "busy, you know. But hey, things change." After he hangs up Joey regrets how the call has gone.

The stress of the first week is taking its toll. His composure is slipping. Joey finds himself muttering to an empty room. "Typical Joey. Joey the loser. Joey who jerks off in fucking parking lots." The room doesn't dignify his outburst with a response.

He doesn't want Dusty to see *that* side of him; the dirty, pervy, pathetic side, the pants-around-the-ankles, humping-a-manicurist-on-a-broken-lawn-chair side, the spasm-of-scary-night-dreams side. He wants Dusty to have a higher opinion of him, to think that he's above the sort of sordid shit typified by the Leonard Spinkles of the world. He wants Dusty to admire him the way he admires Dusty. He dreads that Dusty might divine his fantasy of an arched back, a glistening chest, a blast of cum, and decide that Joey Verona isn't worth his time. So Joey avoids Dusty, praying to a god he doesn't believe in that his obsession will pass.

Over the next few days, the universe conspires against him. Every TV channel seems to be showing a fag movie. Horrors unfold. He switches from *The Birdcage* with Robin Williams, Mork from Ork, as a gay nightclub owner (what would Mindy think!), to *The Broken Hearts Club*, with Joey's childhood hero from "Superman," Dean Cain, showing a different kind of man-steel. Then "Oprah" and her "Queer Eye for the Straight Guy" special and, late at night when Joey is most vulnerable, the worst of them all, "Queer as Folk," with a blow job or naked shower romp in *every* fucking scene. Joey decides not to watch any more television. His mother would be pleased. She always said television was a portal straight to Hades.

He turns to the printed word for solace. He goes to the library to read the newspaper his parents won't allow in the house. The headline story is about *Brokeback Mountain* and cowboy love. Fucking queer *New York Times*. So he heads to the periodicals section, and finds the one magazine surely fag-free, *Californian Shooter*. As he flicks the pages, photos of burly moustachioed lumberjack types with guns propped against their solid thighs—a bleeding buck with gaping mouth and velvety antlers sprawled before them—flash before his eyes. He goes to the bathroom. A mistake. In thick black ink, right over the urinal, someone has written FOR HOT ORAL BE HERE 3PM WEEKDAYS, illustrating his text with a cartoon of a big dick being polished by a square-jawed guy with alarmingly full lips. Joey can't help but think the cocksucker has a striking resemblance to himself. He leaves the library in disgust. Something about books and queers. Where there's one you find the other. "Okay, Lord, I surrender," he says to himself. "You win. Show me what you want me to do. Send me a sign."

Dusty knocks on his door the very next night. Damn. Double damn. He has a six-pack in his hands and a wide, uncomplicated grin on his face. There's nothing Joey can do. He has to let him in. Dusty hops straight onto the bed. Bounces up and down like a kid. Damn. Triple Damn.

Pretty soon, after three beers each—the empty bottles left to clink against each other in the sink, like spent torpedoes—the same sense of ease they shared with each other once, back home, reasserts itself. They talk surf. They talk about Joey's mother's bad taste in Christian rock. They laugh about the time she found incense in Joey's room and thought it was crack.

"Honey," she'd said, a tremor of terror in her voice, "is this *cracked* cocaine?" Like it was in the vein of cracked pepper or something. An illicit condiment.

They reminisce about perfect waves on perfect summer days. Dusty tries to explain his grad study program in biochemistry but Joey doesn't really care. Dusty notices Joey isn't following his account and says, "Don't sweat it, Joey, it's boring crap," and throws an arm around his neck in a mock headlock.

The beer is having its effect. So much so that Joey finds himself wondering what Dusty looks like under his clothes. He'd seen him, when they were in the surf, the broad shoulders, the strong chest with perfectly round nipples, the ridged abs, the muscled arms, the firm back, the solid legs. But now Joey wonders about what the boardshorts had hidden. What would it be like to see another man's privates up close? Would it gross him out or would he like the sight *too* much? Liking it at all would be something. All this is hypothetical anyway. Joey thinks Dusty is just as likely to take out his penis as he is to don a top hat and sing show tunes. It isn't going to happen.

The night wears on and their closeness grows. The alcohol is acting on Joey like Prozac. He hasn't a care in the world. When the old visuals of Dusty pop back into his head, he doesn't try to shoo them away. He lets them be. And when his hard-on rises, he does the same. Lets it happen. Sits with the ache, even enjoying the sensation of his manhood straining against his jeans. He doesn't care at all that another man is the object of his yearning. He's too drunk to care. The tight aching in his pants is enough to erase any anxiety. After all…it *is* Dusty. Soon Joey wonders if he should make a move, put his hand on Dusty's leg. If he doesn't object, move the hand farther up. See what happens.

Then Dusty says he's got to get going. *Has he read my mind?* Joey wonders, but Dusty tells him he has early morning obligations, and it's getting late.

Joey closes the door with a mixture of disappointment and relief. No release from this urge, this itch, but at least he's

saved his straightness. The way things are going his straightness is seriously endangered. Like the Californian wood slug,
like the condor. He undresses, flops into bed, turns out the light,
lies there, lies there as his heart beats, lies there and fights the
onslaught of images: Dusty standing tall before him, his cock
revealed and erect, his chest heaving, groaning again.

He lies there, wills his own dick to go soft, thinks of unsexy
things, potato salad, body odor, Christian rock, Miss June and
her soiled crease. It doesn't work. His dick is raging. He contem-
plates jerking off. Now that he's doing his own laundry, he can
shoot onto his sheets. He tweaks his nipple. Too hard. He yelps.
The stress is getting to him.

"Fuck it!"

He jumps out of bed and turns on the lamp, finds Dusty's
number, the number he was afraid to call when he arrived at the
university, and dials.

"Who the fuck's this?"

"Joey."

"Joe... What's up? It's late. I just left you."

"Can you come back to my room?"

"Why?" He sounds reluctant, but Joey doesn't care.

"I need you for something."

"Can it wait till morning, bro? I'm already undressed for bed."

"I don't think so. No. I need you to come now."

"Okay. But you better be dying or something, Joey...."

Joey hangs up. Freaks out. Moves to call back. Hangs up
again. Catches sight of himself in the mirror. He's lean. Years of
surfing have been good for him. His shoulders are strong and
his stomach is tight, flat. He checks out his dick. Zara said it
was big. But what does she know? Before their sex in the lawn
chair, she was a virgin. He flexes his bicep. A decent bulge. All
that paddling. He calms down. He plans. When Dusty walks in,

he'll get right to it. No fucking around. Straight to the point. See what happens.

Dusty's wearing Adidas track pants and a black duffle coat. His square jaw ignites Joey's desire, that and the solid way he's put together. Dusty shuts the door, smiles at Joey. Joey melts. That smile. He steps toward Dusty, determined to make his move.

Dusty senses something. "What's going on?" Joey doesn't answer. He reaches out instead, unbuttons Dusty's coat. Dusty isn't wearing a shirt. His chest is bare. Smooth and perfect. The nipples erect from the cool air.

Dusty is confused, clearly wondering what the hell is going on. When Joey puts his mouth to Dusty's nipple, comprehension dawns. He steps back, says, "Joe…what the fuck…?" Joey takes the nipple in his mouth again, gives it a nibble, cups Dusty's balls and squeezes gently, all so fast, so smoothly, that Dusty doesn't have time to react before pleasure makes him moan. Joey takes that moan as a signal and, to his own amazement, drops to his knees, pinches Dusty's saliva-soaked nipple with one hand, pulls down the track pants with the other. Dusty isn't wearing under-wear. His dick bobs before Joey's eyes. Without hesitating, spit filling his mouth, he takes in the cock he's dreamt about in his wet dreams, continues to twist Dusty's nipple. Dusty lets out a crazy moan. As if he's never felt so good before.

"Ohh, Joe…."

This feels so natural, thinks Joey. *Not strange, not wicked, as normal as breathing. As American as apple pie.* Joey imagines Dusty a puppet under his control, a sense of power that ignites his adventurous streak. He presses a finger against Dusty's hole. He read in *Playboy*, in Leonard's basement, that this was meant to feel good. To Joey's surprise, his finger is drawn inside the mysterious pucker. Dusty bends his legs, positions himself so that Joey's finger is bumping his prostate, a sensation that thrills both young men. Dusty moans, long moans, he's loving what he's getting.

Joey doesn't really know what he's doing but he keeps the suction on Dusty's penis as best he can, sliding his lips up and down the shaft, taking it in as far as he can so that the head is bumping the back of his throat. Dusty shudders and holds on tighter to Joey's hair. Joey moves his finger in and out of Dusty's flower, taking care to massage the ridged bump in the way *Playboy* suggested, the way that leads to stronger orgasms.

Before long Joey can feel Dusty's dick expand to its limit. Then, almost out of nowhere, Dusty grasps Joey's hair and starts thrusting deep into his mouth. After just a few strokes Dusty shudders and blasts cum down Joey's throat, crying so loudly that everyone in the dorm must hear it. Joey swallows every drop. He keeps licking and nibbling until Dusty has to push him away.

When it's over Dusty falls back onto the bed. Joey catches his breath and then gets up and looks at that body, that face, those eyes half-lidded, that solid chest glimmering with sweat, that mouth emptied of moans. Pants around his ankles. Joey's heart fills with joy. When Dusty's breathing returns to normal he opens his eyes. He fires another one of those smiles at Joey.

"Shit, bro, I'm going to have to pound you good and hard for that," he says.

MISS VEL'S PLACE

Jonathan Asche

The house was so far out in the country that the road to it wasn't even paved, or marked. Nevertheless, it was well traveled, especially on Friday and Saturday nights.

It was a Thursday afternoon when Ford drove down that road and parked in the gravel lot beside the shabby, two-story farmhouse. Brent, who sat in front of him in Algebra II his junior year, told Ford about going here, and how everyone was real nice, but he said if Ford went he should go sometime during the week. They sent away high school kids on Fridays and Saturdays on account some of the customers were afraid they might run into their own sons. The idea of his father coming to such a place gave Ford the shivers.

Ford rang the front doorbell six times, but no one answered. He tried the door, and it was locked. He went around to the back door, thinking maybe that's where he was supposed to go, that a place like this probably didn't want people using the front entrance, even if the house was way out in Bumfuck.

There was no bell on the back door so Ford knocked. When no one answered, Ford knocked harder. He was pounding the door with his fist hard enough to rattle the glass in the windows when someone yelled, "Ain't no one there."

There was a rust-stained house trailer in the yard behind the house, about to be swallowed whole by the kudzu vines creeping up the gully behind it. A young black man in his early twenties stood in the trailer's doorway, grinning, wearing nothing but a pair of red basketball shorts. The waistband fell a few inches below the man's waist, showing off cut muscle and the fact that he wore no underwear. He stepped onto the crumbling cement blocks that served as steps to the trailer's front door, and Ford thought he saw the guy's dick jiggling freely beneath the loose fabric of his shorts.

"Place'll be closed another week," the man said, and Ford jerked his gaze back to his face. "Miss Vel took some of her girls down to the coast. Said all those workmen helping rebuild after that hurricane last month would be a fuckin' gol' mine." The man laughed heartily. "Guess you could call it a business trip."

The news was disappointing, but Ford felt a flush of relief. "I'll come back week after next, then," he said, climbing off the house's back porch.

"Don't have to run off just yet." The man was standing in the middle of the yard now, hands on his hips. It was early October, but fall was slow in coming. The sun turned the man's brown skin bronze where it hit the ridges of his firm muscles, the heat making him shine with sweat. "Got no whores around for you, but you can get a beer for your trouble, maybe even have a smoke if you like." The man winked, letting Ford know he wasn't talking tobacco.

"I don't know," Ford said, taking a couple of steps backward.

"C'mon, I won't bite," the man said, his bright white teeth gleaming.

Ford's eyes fell below the man's waist again, and he saw the head of the man's cock pressing against the fabric of his shorts. Ford barely realized the words were leaving his mouth when he said, "Sure, okay."

Inside, the trailer was cramped and Ford, who everyone said should've gone out for basketball if only he had been better coordinated, had to duck his head to keep from scraping the ceiling. There were dirty dishes in the kitchen sink and the place smelled of bacon grease and pot smoke, but otherwise it was relatively neat, or at least not filthy as Ford had expected it to be, judging from how trashy the trailer looked on the outside.

The man introduced himself. "Orlando. Most folks just call me Lando," he said. "I take care of things for Miss Vel, from fixing toilets to tossing out drunks."

They weren't alone in the trailer. Sitting cross-legged on the living room sofa was a white guy with curly blond hair, about Ford's age, wearing nothing but cutoffs and a slack-jawed expression as he watched some D-grade action movie on TV. He barely acknowledged Ford's presence. Ford recognized him from school.

"That there's Del, Miss Vel's boy—a man, now, I s'pose, but—" Lando shrugged and opened the refrigerator, which had been spray-painted gold. He pulled out two sixteen-ounce cans of beer and handed Ford one. "He's a man where it counts, at least. That'll be five dollars."

Ford hadn't expected to pay for Lando's hospitality, but didn't protest. He was curious what Lando meant about Del being a man "where it counts." Ford had never really talked to Del in school, because Del was in the Special Ed class, and had dropped out in the ninth grade after being arrested, though what for Ford was never quite sure. Depending whom you asked, he was either caught jacking off in public or was busted for blowing guys at a rest stop off Highway 49. Either way, Ford could understand why Del wouldn't want to show his face at school ever again. The guy was already cruelly teased for having a whore for a mother and being in the retard class; a sex scandal on top of that was too much to live down.

Ford took a seat in a cracked vinyl chair, sneaking glances at Del between pulls of his beer. He supposed he was cute, for a mouth-breather. Ford remembered him as scrawny, but now he was about as built-up as Lando, as if Del had spent his time away from school doing hard labor. His eyes were heading for Del's crotch before he could stop himself, and when he heard Lando chuckling he whipped his gaze toward the TV.

Lando was standing at the kitchen entrance, his smile broader than ever. "Like I said, he's a man where it counts. Can show you, if you like."

"Naw, that's okay," Ford said, feeling his face burn.

"Hey, Del, whyn't you show this guy here how big a man you are."

"Huh?" Del sounded as if he'd just been woken from a deep sleep.

"C'mon, show 'im."

"But I'm watchin' TV."

In two steps Lando had crossed the living room and shut off the TV. "Now you can show this guy how big a man you are."

Del looked vacantly at the blank TV screen, still hoping, it seemed, that it would come back on. He got to his feet a few seconds later, and Ford was better able to see his hard torso, see that it was covered with golden hair. When Del undid the top button of his cutoffs, Ford said, "You don't hafta do that," because it was what he thought he should say, not because he meant it.

But whether Ford meant his protest didn't matter. Del's zipper came down regardless, and out came his dick. "See, whatta I tell you?" Lando said. "Good Lord may've shortchanged 'im upstairs but he made up for it down below."

Del did have a big dick, about six or seven inches, soft, and a good size around, too. The kind of dick that got Ford thinking the thoughts that had plagued him since junior high, the kind of thoughts he'd hoped one of Miss Vel's girls would put to rest for good.

"Looks even better hard," Lando said. Ford didn't even have to look at him to tell he was grinning. "Wanna see it stiff? Go on, Del, show this dude what it looks like hard."

"That's..." Ford's protest dried up in his throat. Del started fondling his cock, looking down at his crotch—they were all looking at his crotch. If having everyone's attention made him nervous, Del didn't show it. Ford gulped more beer, hoping the alcohol might dull any possible physical reaction.

Del's prick gradually inflated before their eyes. Ford's own cock responded to the sight, and he crossed his legs, hoping Lando didn't notice. When Del had worked up a semi he looked up, treated them to a goofy grin and giggled. Holding the base of his dick with one hand, Del slapped it into the palm of the other, looking directly at Ford, his grin now an approximation of a seductive smile.

Ford stared at the other man's cock, thicker and longer now, the head succulently plump. The air inside the trailer became thin, breathing requiring more effort than when he first entered. His stomach curdled, his crotch tingled.

Lando said, "He can suck hisself. Wanna see?"

Yes! Out loud, Ford said, "No, I..."

"Sure you do. Only cost twenty dollars."

"I...I don't have that much on me."

"Bullshit. You come to Miss Vel's you gotta have least fifty dollars in your pocket. Del's gonna put on a show for you, and you're gonna pay to see it."

There was an implied "or else" in Lando's words. Ford pulled his wallet from his back pocket and pulled out two tens, trying to hold the wallet so Lando couldn't see the other bills. Lando plucked the money from his hands, thanking him obsequiously.

"Okay, Del," Lando said, holding up the bills. "Show the man your special talent."

Del pulled off his shorts. Completely naked now, he lay down on the sofa. He wasn't smiling anymore, his expression one of concentration, like a circus performer about to do a death-defying stunt. And then Del raised his legs up over his head, his toes touching the end table closest to where his head rested, sending an empty Coke can to the floor. With his body bent in half, his semihard cock was positioned over his face, nearly two inches from his lips. Raising his head, Del closed the distance, his lips locking around the tip of his cockhead.

"Can only suck the head," Lando said. "But that's enough. Can suck hisself 'til he cums, you want."

Ford ignored him, his attention focused on Del slurping his own dick, seeing it getting even harder. Ford was getting harder, too, and crossed his legs, again, hoping to conceal the rising mound in his crotch.

"Ever try and do that ya'self?"

Lando had moved closer, standing immediately to the left of Ford's chair. Annoyed by the intrusion, Ford intended to throw an irritated scowl Lando's way, but surprise pulled his furrowed brows upward when he turned to the pimp wannabe.

The front of Lando's shorts poked out lewdly, the man making no effort to conceal his arousal. "I tried few times," Lando answered his own question. "Never could do it. Most

I managed was jacking off onto my own face. Ever do that?"
Lando grabbed his crotch then, massaging his cock through the
thin material of the shorts, showing his bright white teeth all
the while.

Ford turned away, not answering, and drained his beer. He
rested the empty can between his legs, wanting to ask for another
one but not wanting to speak to Lando, his face burning from
the other man's words, his mind conjuring up a visual of the
muscular black man naked, legs over his head, his white load
splattering his dark brown face. Ford's dick throbbed.

Del's cock was rigid, enabling him to take the entire head
into his mouth. His ass bobbed gently in the air in time to the
steady *slurp-slurp-slurp* of his self-satisfaction. His balls draped
over his fingers where his hand held the base of his cock, rolling
loosely within their fuzzy pink sac. Ford cupped a hand over the
bulge in his jeans, telling himself all he was doing was watching
a freak show, nothing more.

Lando said, "Hey."

Ford turned, then recoiled.

Lando had pulled his shorts down and was waving his dick
in front of Ford. Maybe not as long as Del's—only lacking an
inch or so—but certainly as thick, the dark shaft bumpy with
engorged veins, the head a lighter brown fading to a dusky pink
near the piss-slit. "Ever suck a black man's cock?" he asked.

It was all Ford could do to breathe, let alone speak. "I need to
go," he said, the words coming out in a hoarse gasp. He began
to rise from his seat.

Lando pushed him back down. "I think ya want to stay."

"Hey, Del," Lando called across the narrow room, "how
'bout stoppin' what yer doin', suck something else for a while."

Del kept on sucking his cock until Lando called out to him
again, more forcefully than before. Del stopped then, lowering

his legs until he was lying prone across the sofa, his prick wet
with spit and pulsing visibly. "C'mon, Lando, I's almost done,"
he complained, the words coming out a whiny slur. When he
looked over at Ford and Lando, though, he got that goofy grin
again and got up, lumbering, zombielike, toward Lando—or,
more specifically, Lando's cock.

"Show our new friend how you like to suck other dicks,"
Lando said, though Del was dropping to his knees unasked,
grinning, saliva dribbling on his chin. He took hold of the other
man's hard-on, gave the shaft a squeeze, and rubbed the head
across his lower lip. He flicked the slit with his tongue, and then
licked the cockhead like it was a chocolate lollipop. Finally, he
took Lando's dick into his mouth.

Ford had seen his share of straight porn, but he'd gotten a
few peeks at gay porn on the Internet—rather than buy Ford his
own computer, his parents had purchased one for the family and
set it up in the living room. It was a challenge to look up information for a history report without being interrupted; visiting a
porn site for more than a few minutes was out of the question.
Now, seeing Del suck Lando's cock two feet in front of him,
Ford was paralyzed by contradictory feelings. His cock was so
hard it hurt yet terror gripped his insides so tightly he thought
he might hyperventilate.

Del swallowed Lando's rod whole. Lando, groaning loudly,
grabbed a fistful of Del's hair, holding it like a saddle horn and
thrusting his hips forward, fucking Del's mouth. His blond
friend didn't gag once.

"How 'bout it?" Lando drawled, rolling his head toward
Ford. "Wanna give it a taste now?"

"I don't...I mean, I'm not..."

"*Shee*-it," Lando chuckled. "You scared, is what you is. Tell
you what, you suck me and I'll have Del suck you for free."

Ford stared at Del's lips locked around the base of Lando's cock, his nose cushioned in the other man's tightly curled pubes, his hand cupping Lando's balls. Ford tried to imagine that was *his* mouth wrapped around that dick, that Lando was holding *him* by the hair. But he couldn't conjure the image. Even in his own fantasies, Ford was never one of the players; he was too afraid of confronting the truth even within the privacy of his own mind. Del's mouth around his cock, though, was too strong a temptation to resist.

"H-how much?" Ford asked.

"Hey-hey-hey—ease up there," Lando said, pushing Del away, taking deep breaths. "Taking me farther than I wanna go just yet." To Ford, he said, "What's that you said?"

"How much? For Del to…to suck me."

Lando flashed his teeth. "Another twenty, but free if you suck me. You want, you can fuck his ass. Better than pussy, all tight an' shit. Del, he likes that almost as much as suckin' dick. I'd offer you both, but I don't think you'll last long enough. Probably cum second you stick it in, no matter which hole it is."

Ford's cock throbbed an affirmative.

"So, you want it for free or you gonna pay?"

Wade pulled his wallet from his back pocket for the third time since entering the trailer. "I…I'll pay for it."

"Suit yerself," Lando shrugged.

After Ford gave him a twenty, Lando asked if he wanted to get a blow job or to fuck Del. The sight of Del gulping down Lando's cock burned into his brain, Ford chose the blow job.

"Then I'll take the ass. Hear that, Del? You gonna get filled up on both ends."

Del sat on his haunches, idly stroking his boner, smiling mindlessly.

Lando pulled off his shorts and tossed them across the room.

"Gotta get our stuff. Don't y'all start without me," he said, starting down the trailer's claustrophobic hallway.

"Gonna get outta yer clothes?" It was the first time Del had spoken directly to Ford since he entered the trailer.

"I thought Lando said—"

Del leaned forward, placing a hand on Ford's knee. His other hand reached for the empty beer can nestled between Ford's legs. "You gotta big dick?" Del dropped the can to the floor and grabbed Ford's crotch.

An electric heat passed from Del's hand through Ford's jeans; he jerked upright, suddenly as rigid as his cock. Ford's breathing quickened and his lips quivered, trying to form words he couldn't find.

"Boy, you not undressed *yet*?" Lando had returned, holding a bottle of lubricant and foil-wrapped condoms.

"I—"

"Well, go *on*!"

Ford stood uneasily, doing his best not to look at the other two men. He took off his shoes and pants. He was going to leave his T-shirt on until Lando said, "You see either of *us* wearin' a shirt?" Ford turned away so he was facing neither Lando nor Del, not wanting to see their reactions when he pulled down his white cotton briefs to reveal his hard-on.

It didn't matter. "How 'bout that Del?" Lando cackled. "Not bad, not bad a'tall."

Ford sat back down. Del was still kneeling on the floor, waiting.

Ford gripped the chair's armrests, bracing himself.

Del gripped Ford's cock.

Pleasure crackled beneath Ford's skin. He looked down at Del regarding his cock, his hand gently stroking it. He paused, looking up at Ford. He no longer looked vacant. With

Ford's stiff pole in his hand, Del exuded absolute confidence. Ford saw Lando kneeling behind Del, holding his latex-covered cock in one hand, his other hand playing with Del's ass. Del closed his mouth over Ford's prick, and Ford's eyes slammed shut. Excitement rocketed through his body with such force that he sucked in his breath and threw his head back, as if he was enduring the rapid drops and twists of a roller coaster. The warm, moist cavern of Del's mouth, his wriggling tongue against Ford's cockhead—it was better than Ford had ever imagined.

Keeping his eyes closed, Ford tried to imagine it was a girl sucking him, first trying to picture one of the girls he knew, like Shayla, who graduated in his class and now worked part-time as receptionist at the packaging plant where he worked. He tried to conjure her face, her body, but though he thought she was pretty, he never thought of her "that way." He tried visualizing celebrities, women who clearly wanted to be thought of "that way," but it was difficult imagining them doing to him what Del was doing. Worse, trying to picture a woman made his boner go slack.

Opening his eyes, Ford looked down between his legs and watched Del swallow his dick, slurping loudly, spit bubbling out of his lips and dripping off Ford's shaft. Del pulled his mouth away, grunting as his body pitched forward. Lando was mounting him.

Ford saw the dark-skinned man leaning into Del's ass, his hands clutched around the simpleton's waist, eyes half-closed, whispering: "Better than pussy."

Ford's hard-on was revived.

Del gulped down Ford's cock, his head bobbing in rhythm to Lando's thrusts. Ford pushed his hips upward, working against the descent of Del's mouth onto his dick, his cockhead hitting the back of Del's throat. Ford fought the urge to run his fingers through Del's hair, clutching the chair's armrests the whole time, as if he were struggling to keep from being ejected from his seat.

The sensation intensified, until pleasure could no longer be contained. Ford struggled to ride the rapturous feeling a while longer, but he couldn't fight it. Emitting a ragged gasp, his body jerking in his chair, he came.

Del greedily gulped down his load, squeezing the shaft of Ford's dick to push out every last drop. Even when Ford thought he was drained, a few more beads of cum oozed out of his piss-slit, lapped up happily by Del.

Weakened by his orgasm, Ford sat, motionless, not quite believing he'd participated in what had happened. In his dazed state he watched Del, his face shiny with saliva, sweat and cum, sit up and lean against Lando's chest. Del's oversized dong was bobbing in the air, a clear thread of precum swinging off the head.

Lando reached around and grabbed Del's dick, pulling on it while he fucked him in hard, sharp stabs. He was looking over Del's shoulder, whispering something to him while looking directly at Ford, his eyes knowing.

Ford told himself he should look away, but he couldn't. He couldn't take his eyes off Del's writhing body, his big, drooling cock. He couldn't help but stare at the contrast of Lando's chocolate skin against Del's whiteness.

The two men came within seconds of each other. Del was first, his cumshot rocketing straight up, splattering his own heaving chest. Ford was sure Lando would've said something about that—in his mind he could hear him whistling, saying, "How 'bout that?"—if he weren't so close to cumming himself. Lando was really fucking Del hard, his thrusts making Miss Vel's son bounce and sway like a rag doll in a windstorm. His face was screwed up, his lips trembling. Ford expected Lando to roar like a lion when he got off. Instead, Lando let out a coughing gasp, his body convulsing as he came. Del rolled his hips, massaging Lando's throbbing pole with his ass.

Del turned his head and stuck out his tongue. Lando leaned in and met him, the two men kissing awkwardly, Lando tweaking one of Del's sticky nipples as their tongues dueled.

Lando looked at Ford, and their eyes met. He smiled conspiratorially.

Ford hopped up from his seat then, rushing to gather his clothes, getting dressed hurriedly. By the time he got his clothes on, Lando and Del had settled onto the sofa. Neither of them had bothered to get dressed. Ford headed for the door.

"Maybe next time you won't be so shy," Lando called after him.

Ford paused at the door, looking over at the couple on the couch. He shook his head. "I ain't queer like you," he said. He opened the door and rushed out of the trailer, trying to outrun Lando's deep, rumbling guffaw.

On the drive home he wondered what it would be like to suck a black man's dick and to fuck Del up the ass.

ORBS

Clarence Wong

I couldn't take my eyes off them. Two silver balls, one on each side of the crown of his penis, held together by a slender rod pierced through the base of the crown. They shone in the San Diego sunlight, a beacon in the sea of pink and beige bodies lying buttocks up on the beach.

"They're from Tiffany," said Colin, later, flipping up his penis and showing me the tiny mark embossed on the silver rod.

"Tiffany sells this kind of...uh...jewelry?" I said, trying to hide my surprise.

"Special order," he said. "I know people there."

I was taking the summer off from my regular job teaching English to Mexican immigrants. I spent my days reading Hemingway on Black's Beach, the far, secluded end where gay men sunbathed in the nude under the stern eye of state park rangers.

To pay the rent, I worked the dinner shift at House of Hunan. Mr. Yang, the owner, had hired me on the spot. I satisfied the two requirements he had for waiters. They had to be Chinese and they had to speak English. House of Hunan's clientele was exclusively Western. No self-respecting Chinese would eat there. The fare was strictly middle-American versions of Chinese food. Everything was served in the same brown, gooey sauce.

Colin was an Aussie from Brisbane, currently living in Amsterdam. Short and stocky, he had sun-bleached hair and a shapely goatee. His forearms bulged like Popeye's. To me, he looked like a wrestler from the Ukrainian team at the Olympics. Or a short-order cook at an all-night diner. I couldn't decide which.

All this came later. That day on Black's Beach, Colin and I did not converse. Our eyes did not meet. I was too shy. I kept my eyes lowered, fixed on the two silver orbs flanking the ruddy knob of his penis. I was transfixed by the sight.

Our eyes met that night at Club San Diego, the city's liveliest bathhouse. I couldn't really afford the admission fee, but it was Saturday night and I needed to be elevated from my shift at House of Hunan. Besides, I had an inkling I would see Colin there.

I found him in the steam room. In the misty half-light, the silver orbs glowed softly, guiding me like a lighthouse. Colin sat on the top bleacher, thighs apart, towel at his feet. His hair was slicked back and his goatee glistened with droplets of sweat. A duet of Latin men, smooth and lean, hung on either side of him. Their bodies formed a tight knot of limbs and lust.

I sidled into the room, pretending to mind my own business, but it was hard to ignore the heat emanating from Colin and the Latin lovers. I shifted my eyes to peek at them.

Colin was looking right at me. He held out his hand in a gesture of welcome. As though under a spell, I walked toward him. Colin's outstretched hand yanked off my towel. Then, grasping my buttocks, he pulled me forward. At the same time, the Latin pair enfolded me with their arms. I was absorbed into a vortex of heat.

Sex with three men is at least three times as pleasurable as sex with one man. There are thrice the number of tongues, thrice the number of fingers to act as instruments of arousal and stimulation. My body exploded with sensations.

Colin leaned in and tried to kiss me. I pulled away. That was my rule. No kissing. The bathhouse was for sex: casual, anonymous, impersonal sex. It was not the place for intimacy or romance. Kissing, while undeniably sexual, hinted at intimacy and flirted with the possibility of romance. Therefore, no kissing.

That's not to say I didn't want to kiss Colin. On the contrary, I longed to kiss him. His breath was warm and sweet and perfumed with tobacco. I had a mere week before given up smoking. I would've given anything to put my mouth on his and suck the nicotine out of his lungs.

"You know," said Vijay, my counselor at the community health clinic, "kissing is not against the program. You're allowed to kiss, even if he's a smoker."

"No," I said, "no kissing at the bathhouse. That's the rule."

We all came, all four of us. Colin came first. He was the leader of our little ménage, the first violin of our quartet. He chose our positions and determined the pace of our playing. For people who were strangers to each other, we played together with remarkable synchronicity.

I came next, my eyes closed, hissing softly through my teeth, my hands clasping Colin's. In the third and final act, the Latin duo brought our playing to a crescendo. To my everlasting amazement, they came together at the exact same moment. I may be wrong, but I got the sense they had practiced this many times before, not that this in any way diminished my awe at their prowess.

There are men who get their money's worth at the bathhouse. They arrive early, stay all night, and enjoy a full sampling of the treats offered that evening. I am not one of these men. I leave immediately after I come, if I am lucky enough to come.

"Going already?"

I turned to see Colin saunter into the narrow locker room. I struggled into my jacket and slammed the locker door shut.

"I'm Colin, by the way. You are…?"

I smiled politely but said nothing. No names at the bathhouse. That was another rule. No *let's have dinner next week*.

Colin smiled back. "No worries, I understand." He reached into his locker and fished out a pack of Marlboros. "Got a light?"

I stuck my hand into the back pocket of my Levi's and, sure enough, there it was, the box of matches I always carried.

"Keep it," I said, tossing the red and white box with House of Hunan printed on it over to Colin. "I quit last week."

"Better you than me," said Colin, lighting up.

"You can't smoke in here."

"I know," said Colin, giving me a good-humored wink. "My bad."

He turned and headed out of the room, swinging his hips and blowing smoke rings in the air.

House of Hunan was dead. A late summer storm had brought down lashings of rain and sent the street litter scuttling along the sidewalk. Normally, on a night like this, Manuel the busboy and I would hang out in the kitchen sharing a pack of smokes.

Since I'd quit two weeks ago, Manuel was too kindhearted to
smoke in front of me. Instead, we sat at the rickety kitchen
table chatting companionably while we helped Cook remove
the tails from bean sprouts piled high on the table. We were so
engrossed in our banter we did not hear the chime of the front
doorbell. Seconds later, Mr. Yang stuck his head in and growled,
"Customer, table four."

Colin sat alone in the musty dining room. He was dressed in
a San Diego Padres sweatshirt, jeans, and a pair of flip-flops. His
jeans were sodden from ankle to knee. Behind him against the
wall stood a long, sleek surfboard.

"Hello," he said, eyes widening in surprise, "I didn't know
you work here." He dug in his pocket and held up the box
of matches I'd given him a week ago. "I was in the mood for
Chinese."

"What can I get you?" I said, hoping I didn't sound too
unfriendly. No fraternizing with tricks from the bathhouse.
Another rule.

"You're very attached to your rules," said Vijay during one of
my visits to the clinic.

"We all need rules to live by."

"Why?"

I was nonplussed. "Because without rules, life would be…"

"What?"

"Chaotic."

"A little chaos can be good for the soul."

I snorted. I liked Vijay but, at times, he could be pedantic in
an insufferable, Deepak Chopra sort of way.

"What do you recommend?" said Colin, scanning the menu.

"The cheeseburger at Leticia's across the street."

Colin laughed. "Funny. But seriously..."

"I'm serious."

Colin eyed me for a second. "What, you don't want me to eat here?"

I shrugged. "It's a free country."

"How about we make a deal? I'll go across to Leticia's if you'll join me there."

"No, I..."

"C'mon, where's the harm? Burger, fries and beer. Say yes."

I cast a wary eye at Mr. Yang behind the cash register. He did not approve of chatting with the customers.

"All right, one beer. I get off in thirty minutes."

"Attaboy!" Colin pushed back from the table and started gathering up his gear.

I picked up the menu from the table and walked back to the kitchen. On the way, I said to Mr. Yang, "Changed his mind. What can you do? Assholes, some people."

"I saw you at Black's last week," I said, practically shouting. Leticia's was packed in spite of the storm.

"I saw you too. You were checking out my balls."

"Oh..." I felt myself blushing up to the tips of my ears.

"No worries, everybody checks them out."

"Did they...did it hurt a lot, getting your dick pierced?"

"A little."

"Why did you do it?"

"No particular reason. I guess because everybody said not to."

I was more curious than ever. "Have you had any trouble with them? Rust, infection, getting them caught in your zipper?"

"Nope, nothing like that. Only spot of trouble is at the airport. Metal detectors. Sets them off every time."

"That's a pain."

"Actually, in my line of work, that could be rather useful."

Colin, it turned out, was a smuggler. He was hired by clients to carry illegal Brazilian emeralds from Tijuana to Amsterdam.

"What are illegal emeralds?" I asked.

"Emeralds not certified by the cartel. Officially, the idea is to certify the quality of the stones, but in fact it's just a scam to keep supply low and prices high. I carry illegal stones to Amsterdam that aren't allowed in because they have no certificates."

"Is it dangerous?"

"Only if I get caught." Colin laughed. "Twenty-five years in jail. That's where my balls come in handy. They set off the metal detectors and the security goons get so flustered when they find my balls they forget to search the rest of me. I've been doing this for ten years. Fuck, everybody deals in illegal stones."

The contours of his penis and orbs showed clearly through the denim of his jeans. Colin rubbed himself enticingly. Leaning over, he whispered, "Let's go back to my hotel."

I instinctively shook my head. No going back to hotels. But we'd had three rounds of beer. We were both a little tipsy and more than a little aroused.

I had an idea. Colin paid the bill and I led him across the street to the back door of House of Hunan. The kitchen was dark. Manuel had finished cleaning and locked up hours ago.

In the dark, I took Colin's hand and guided him to the anteroom where Cook stored ten-pound bags of onions and garlic. We tore off our clothes. Naked, Colin's mouth worked its way from my neck down to my nipples, then down to my crotch, and back up again. He kissed my nose, my chin. Licking softly, he hovered over my mouth, breathing lightly. I sighed, inhaling the warm smell of tobacco and beer. Then, I turned my head away. Rules were rules.

"Okay, no worries," said Colin good-naturedly. He pushed

me down until I was supine on a bed of garlic and resumed working his mouth up and down my body.

This time, I came first.

Tubes flowed like rivulets into different parts of Colin's body. The hospital room was unnervingly still. The only sounds were the intermittent beep of the heart monitor and the almost inaudible drip-drip-drip of the iv machine.

The ER nurse had called me at House of Hunan. "He named you as next-of-kin," she said. "It's our policy to notify you after surgery."

At first I was annoyed. Colin named *me* next-of-kin? That was presumptuous. We fucked a couple of times. That hardly qualified me as next-of-kin.

Then it dawned on me. He was a visitor. I was probably the only person he knew in San Diego. Well, sort of knew.

"I hope you don't mind," said Colin. His blond hair was darkening and his goatee had lost its shapeliness. "They kept bugging me for my next-of-kin."

"I don't mind," I said.

"You were the only person I could think of."

"It's cool."

Colin looked wan but he was happy to have a visitor.

"Well," I said, struggling to keep up the flow of conversation, "the nurse said something about a surfing accident?"

"Yeah," said Colin, brightening up, "it was a mother of a wave. I thought I had it licked, but I miscalculated. Must have thrown me ten feet in the air. I hit the water in the worst possible way, with my back."

"How are you feeling now?" I asked.

"They tell me I'll live." He didn't say the wave had snapped several of his vertebrae or that they had almost lost him on the operating table. I learned that from the nurse.

"You'll get through this," I said. "I know you will."

"Yes, of course." But his tone did not match the confidence of his words. His eyes clouded over and he looked away.

"Are you afraid you'll...you're not about to die, you know."

"I know."

"What is it then?"

"You don't need to get involved with my problems."

"I'm already involved."

Colin was silent for a long minute. Then he said, "I don't know how I'm going to manage the hospital bill. I don't have any insurance."

I hadn't thought of that.

"The pickup is tomorrow in Tijuana. I'm going to miss it, so I won't get paid."

I looked at Colin aghast. Here was chaos of the first order.

"What are you going to do?"

"There's nothing I can do."

"Would the pickup cover the hospital bill?"

"A big chunk of it. One thing I will say," Colin said with a weak smile, "money's good in the stones business."

The room fell silent. Colin was wrapped up in worry while I struggled with myself. Why was I even bothering? I hardly knew the guy. He was nice and all, but this was not my problem.

And yet, I was getting a little weary of my problem-free life. I had made all these rules just so I wouldn't have any problems, wouldn't be besieged with any of the headaches of romance, love, couplehood. It had felt like a good formula in the beginning, but, in truth, life without problems was a tad empty.

"How about I pick up the stones for you?" I heard myself saying.

"What? You're crazy, no way!" said Colin.

"Why not?"

"Because this is my problem, not yours."

"I'd like to help."

"Not like that! I'm the smuggler, not you."

"But you can't do it tomorrow, I can."

"Look, I know you mean well, but there's no way I'd let you do this. It's dangerous. You could get caught."

"You've been doing this ten years and you haven't been caught."

"That doesn't mean..."

"Colin, let me help. I want to do this."

"Why?"

"Because it'd be fun."

Colin's eyes narrowed. He fixed his gaze on me and searched my face for a long time. I looked steadily back at him, noticing for the first time that his eyes were pale green with flecks of gold.

Finally, he let out a sigh. "All right, I think you're crazy, but if you're sure..."

"I'm sure."

"You'd be saving my ass. I don't know what to say."

"Don't say anything. Just tell me where to go tomorrow."

Colin scribbled the address on a piece of paper and handed it to me. "Be there at noon sharp. Don't carry a backpack, don't carry anything."

I nodded. "Will they give the stones to me? They're expecting you, not me."

Colin pondered this for a moment. Then, he slid open the drawer of the nightstand, removed an article and thrust it into my hand.

I opened my palm and looked into it. There, sitting snugly in the hollow, was a pair of silver balls.

"Show them my balls," said Colin, chuckling. "They'll know I sent you."

The departure hall teemed with Dutch tourists wearing Mexican jewelry and California tans. Colin stood next to me, smiling benignly at the hurly-burly around us. His hair had grown long during his two-month stay at the hospital. Thick and wavy, it hung loosely around his shoulders. His goatee had regained its shapeliness. Trimming it was the first thing Colin attended to upon hearing murmurings among the doctors of his discharge.

Colin traveled light. He checked no luggage. He never does, he told me. He shouldered a leather duffle bag and a Mexican cloth pouch was strapped around his waist.

I missed him already.

"I'll be back, you know," he said.

"I know." I longed to ask when exactly, but I refrained.

"I know I've said this already, but you saved my butt. I don't know how to thank you."

"You don't need to."

"You had fun?"

"I had a blast."

The address in Tijuana he had given me was in a part of town no tourist would dream of venturing into. The air was thick with dust and heavy with humidity. Mosquitoes glided languidly in the dank corners wedged between the tumbling down houses.

None of this made an impression on me. I was so intoxicated with adrenaline, so charged up with the pickup, I could have been on a glacier in Alaska for all the impact my surroundings made on me that day.

The pickup fulfilled every suspense thriller fantasy I had. A man with a narrow, pockmarked face had answered the door. He wore heavy black shades even though the interior of the house was shrouded in darkness. His hands were empty but a heavy blunt object bulged menacingly under his jacket.

He said not a word to me the entire time, merely grunted when I showed him the silver balls. Receding behind filthy brown curtains, he left me alone in the windowless room, bare except for a wooden crucifix hanging on the wall. A few minutes later, he reappeared, handing me a slim white envelope sealed with many layers of duct tape. I was then escorted to the front door.

It had been sublimely cool inside the house, but as I stepped out into the murky sunlight, I noticed my armpits were soaked.

"I should get going," said Colin. "It takes forever to get through security these days."

I nodded, not trusting myself to speak. Colin stepped closer, leaning in until his face was next to mine. Holding my gaze, he brushed his lips lightly over mine.

This time, I yielded. I kissed him back, letting my tongue touch his, savoring the taste of the stick of Marlboro he had smoked in the car on the way to the airport and the sweetness of the man. With our eyes closed, we kissed slowly as if we had all the time in the world.

He kissed and kissed, and I kissed back, making up for all the times I had longed to kiss him but had not allowed myself to. And then I let him go. I let him pick up his duffle bag, give me one last kiss, and join the line at the security checkpoint.

I stood and waited while he inched his way toward the X-ray machine and the metal detector, not wanting to lose the last few moments when we could still exchange smiles. I waited until he deposited his duffle bag and pouch on the conveyor belt of the X-ray machine and stepped through the metal detector.

As expected, the alarm went off, sending a pair of uniformed guards scurrying toward him. Brandishing detector wands, they pulled him aside and herded him behind a curtained off area, but not before Colin was able to turn back and give me one last smile.

I left after that, kicked up my heels and headed home. Vijay had been right. At that moment, my soul was feeling pretty darn good.

INTIMACY

Drew Gummerson

But why me?" I asked.

I was sitting at the desk on the opposite side of the captain. The captain was a large corpulent man given to sudden bouts of anger. The other officers said it was best to butter him up, but I had always found him very fair, without having to slip into sycophancy.

"Why can't Simmons go?" I said. "Or Dorchester?"

The captain raised his hands once from the desk and dropped them again, palms first. It was a gesture of irritation.

"If the face fits," he said.

He pushed an orange oblong pouch toward me.

"The plane leaves at seven A.M. Don't miss it. Be at the airport at least two hours beforehand." He made a show of looking at his watch. "Perhaps three." He gave a little laugh. "We don't want any mishaps, do we? I want to show our Polish brethren what a tight little force we run here. Our reputation for efficacy runs right throughout the EC."

I picked up the pouch and stood from the desk. As my hand was on the door to leave the captain called me back.

"And no funny business," he said. "There's talk."

That night in the barracks I lay awake. The captain's words echoed in my head. "Funny business" were the ones that reverberated. They seemed such a strange choice, ones laid down almost as a gauntlet.

Over by the window, under the gentle glare of a low-wattage bulb, the other officers sat playing cards. They were wearing only underpants and because today was a Tuesday, and underpants were changed on Wednesdays, at 0945, the pants were more than usually stained.

There was the sound of a card being laid down followed by others. Finally, a number of cards were gathered up.

I never joined in these games. It wasn't that congenitally I was a loner, it was more that I liked my own company. If I had been one of those true outsiders, I would have joined a profession that would have allowed me, more often than not, to be on my own; a traveling salesman, or a farmer on a remote oyster farm somewhere.

Another card was laid down, then another, and then I looked at my watch and it was past midnight and I needed to urinate. As I was making my way back to my bed I was stopped short by a burst of conversation that was obviously directed at me. I turned and found myself eye to eye with Dorchester.

"So, you're going to Poland."

It wasn't a question, more a statement of fact, so I merely nodded and made my way back to my bed.

"Hey, you fancy a game?"

I paused for a moment and then, thinking that as I was due at the airport in only a few hours and sleep seemed far away, just this once I might as well join the group.

Simmons collected the cards up and dealt them out again. He had a neat way of doing things that belied his farmhand origins.

"I've heard about Polish women," said Dorchester. "Large thighs and big tits."

"I think that's Russian women," said Smith. "At least, that's what I've heard."

"Shit cards," said Dorchester. "Simmons. It's your start, I think."

The game moved at a frenetic pace. Pretty soon I found myself the only one holding any cards.

"You win," said Dorchester to me. He put his hand down the front of his pants and scratched furiously. "And you were last, Smith. Take your pants off."

Smith looked as if he was about to say something rude but then he merely glared at Dorchester and shrugged. "It's shit," he said.

"Okay," said Dorchester. "Two fingers."

"Two?" said Smith. Now he was angry.

"We always double up in the last game," said Dorchester. "You know the rules."

"But you didn't actually say it was the last game," said Smith.

Now Johnson piped up for the first time. "It *is* getting on. Come on. We all need our sleep. Don't be a spoilsport."

Smith looked like he had a lot to say to this but as obviously everyone was against him he lowered his pants and bent over.

I knew what to do from my nights lying awake in bed. I sucked both fingers and placed them against Smith's sphincter.

"Hurry up," said Johnson. "Don't be scared. He hasn't used it for anything except a couple of farts all night."

With a giving of skin I pushed inside. The sensation was at

once both of physical connection and emotional distance.

"Thirty seconds," said Dorchester. "Twenty-nine, twenty-eight, twenty-seven…"

"Give it a bit of wellie," said Simmons. "See if you can bend your fingers. Smith's had a whole fist up there before."

"Fuck off, Simmons," said Smith.

"Now now," said Johnson. "Take it like a man. You know the rules."

"Ten," said Dorchester, "nine, eight, seven…"

"It hurts like shit," said Smith.

"Like shit," said Johnson, smiling. "I like that."

"Three," said Dorchester, "two, one."

With a sucking sound, I pulled out my fingers. Smith let out a sigh. I looked around for a towel and again found myself locking eyes with Dorchester.

"So you're going to Poland," he said. "It makes me wonder why they chose you. That's what I'm thinking, why *did* they choose you?"

And then, as if as one and it was all prearranged, the four of them leapt up. I felt myself falling back and they were on top of me and I felt my dirtied fingers being pushed into my mouth.

The taste was acrid, as was the smell.

The man on the plane next to me was both very tall and very fat. He was holding a large broadsheet newspaper, the pages of which brushed against me each time he turned a page.

I was in that space between sleep and wakefulness when I realized the man was speaking to me.

"Your first time in Poland?"

I nodded, hopeful that this lack of verbal communication would dissuade any more attempts at what would no doubt be inane conversation.

"Quite a time to be going, what with all this happening...."

I noticed that he had folded the newspaper into a perfect square, highlighting a particular story. The words were in Polish.

"This serial killer has struck again. Always the same, always young men and always he cuts off their penises."

"Penises?" I sat up straighter and felt my scrotum retract itself in my underpants.

"The penises are never found," said the man. "Some say he keeps them as trophies. Others say it is not the penis he revels in, merely the act of cutting. Still others say he eats them. Of course, Poland is a very Catholic country."

"What?" I was surprised at this change of tack.

"If you repress," said the man, "then it will come out in other ways. Look at the Pope. And Al Qaeda, it's the same."

I asked what he meant by this but he wouldn't say anything more. Instead he unfolded the newspaper and moved on to the next story.

Sergeant Drogovich was waiting for me at the airport. I recognized him straightaway, both from the uniform he was wearing and the sign he was holding with my name scrawled across it. The spelling was incorrect.

I guessed Sergeant Drogovich was roughly the same age as me, late twenties, but at the same time, he had a face that was difficult to pin an age on, having a large bushy moustache extending all the way along his upper lip and ending at little points on each side. There was something cavalier about this that I liked.

We shook hands and he led me out to a small, pale blue car. I had seen its like before in early seventies British spy films set almost entirely in the Eastern Bloc. Inside it smelt of petrol and vodka and indeed I could see a bottle neck poking out of the glove compartment.

"We'll go straight to the training ground," said Sergeant Drogovich, "introduce you to the boys and after we can drop off your luggage. I'm putting you up, is that okay? I don't know if they informed you of the accommodation arrangements."

I nodded my head okay and gazed out of the window. I had expected everything to be gray but it wasn't. Tall buildings loomed impressively showing blank windows to the world.

"What exactly is it that I'll be doing?" I asked. The captain had been somewhat stony faced about the actual nature of my assignment.

"Cycling proficiency," said Sergeant Drogovich. "And call me Petr. Except in front of the lads, okay?"

"Cycling proficiency?"

"As a force we've invested quite some money in our cycle task force. We can't afford to let anything go wrong. You are a keen cyclist, I take it?"

Outside four women dressed in black lay a perfectly cylindrical bouquet of flowers at what appeared to me to be a random spot on the pavement.

"Oh yes," I said, "quite keen." Although, in reality, it was quite some time since I had ridden a bike at all.

The lads numbered eight in total. Each was dressed in a neat white T-shirt and tight black trousers that showed off powerful thighs. Overhead, clouds were gathering and the wind had picked up. As Sergeant Drogovich—Petr—spoke to me, some of his words seemed to be carried away across the field.

"Eight weeks on step machines, then we moved on to the bikes themselves. We got them from the Dutch. Since we've joined the EU we've seen all sorts of benefits. Of course, the communist press often made digs about the wastefulness of Western policies, the butter mountain and all that, but it seems the last laugh is on us."

"Sorry?" I said.

"The Dutch donated the bikes. Seems they are from the bike mountain. As opposed to mountain bikes."

I wondered if this was a joke, then I said, "But you said you've invested a lot of money."

Petr moved his hand up to his moustache. "In the training. And recruiting these guys, they are the cream of the crop. A bicycle task force. We will be the envy of the rest of Europe."

It seemed that that was the end of the speech, for Petr reached into his pocket and took out a large blue whistle. He blew into it three times and the lads turned and jogged off to a wooden shed I hadn't noticed before on the edge of the field.

"That's where we keep the bikes," said Petr. "It's quite secure. It's guarded by a dog. She's a bitch and very ferocious. There's a lot riding on this project. No stone has been left unturned."

"How do you get them to train so hard?" I said.

I had hardly needed to blow the whistle Petr had given me. I was amazed at the eight lads' enthusiasm, never having seen a group of people cycle with such verve.

"What is it you people say?" said Petr. "The proof is in the pudding. Look. Today, Ivan is last."

I had noticed that as the lads were completing each of the cycle tasks we set them Petr had been making notes in a little hardback book he carried. I could now see that the notes were in a series of tables, or more precisely, a set of numbers entered onto these tables.

"Wait here," said Petr.

The lads were huddled in a group. While earlier they had

been laughing, boisterous even, now the silence of expectation had fallen over them. Petr opened up the book and puffs of frosted air appeared from his mouth which indicated he was speaking, although because of his moustache, I was not actually able to see his lips move.

As the puffs stopped all of the lads bar one leapt into the air and there was much laughing and clapping of hands. The single remaining boy, Ivan I guessed, looked disconsolate and with a stamp of his feet made his way solitarily to the bike shed. Intrigued by what was happening I moved toward the group.

"Sergeant Drogovich," I started to say but Petr held up a hand to silence me.

"There is something of a ceremony about this," he said and gave a laugh. "We *are* a Catholic country, after all."

It took me a moment to realize what was different about the bike Ivan was wheeling out of the shed, and then I noticed the seat. Instead of the usual triangular leather design, there was a large purple phallus.

Petr leant over and whispered in my ear. "This one came from the Dutch sex museum. Another donation. We didn't have this kind of thing under communism. We much more had to just 'make do.'"

The lads had formed a circle and into the center of this Ivan wheeled the bike. The earlier jollity had now been replaced by a somber silence. Ivan looked toward Petr, perhaps hoping for some kind of reprieve, but as none was apparently forthcoming, he carefully laid down the bike and removed his clothes item by item.

His body was perfectly white, almost marblelike, and as defined as a statue. Petr had stated they were cream of the crop and I wondered under what conditions exactly they were recruited. The clouds had moved in closer and it was about dark.

"If you would, as our guest, do the honors," said Petr and he passed me an open tub of what I guessed must be some kind of lubricant.

Ivan had cupped his hands over his penis and as I approached he turned slightly and bent at the waist, offering up his backside.

I thought how it was only the night before when I had put my fingers up Smith's arse. And here I was again.

"If I put a lot on," I whispered, "it won't hurt so much."

Ivan nodded very slightly. "Thank you," he said. "You are very kind."

We were back in the car and Petr was talking although my mind was elsewhere. I was thinking of Ivan as he sat on the phallus, the way once it was inside him, it looked like he was riding a regular bike. I recalled the officers back at the barracks putting their fingers up each other's arses on a nightly basis under the guise of a game. Everything was something under something else and I was trying to decipher the exact significance of this, if indeed there was any, when I realized the car had stopped and Petr was saying something to me.

"A drink before we return home?"

On each side of the car loomed the gray façades of three-storey buildings. The street was empty and I noticed a gentle snow had started to fall. Flakes were clinging like tiny white insects to the windscreen of the car.

"A regular haunt of mine," said Petr. "I'm sure you'll like it."

My eyes were heavy but it seemed the drink was already a foregone conclusion, like everything else that had happened over the previous two days.

I followed Petr out of the car and up to an unobtrusive iron gate. Petr pushed a button, a buzzer sounded and we gained

access to a courtyard. At the end of this was a staircase, hewn
from the concrete, leading down to a door.

"I found this place quite by chance," said Petr and he rapped
on the door with his knuckles.

The door was opened by a burly man in a thick, ribbed
jumper. From inside I sensed a warm fug of smoke, the cozy
chatter of intimate friends and the gentle beat of music.

The ceiling was not much higher than my own head, and radi-
ating from the main body of the bar were a number of alcoves.
We were led to one of these and within seconds two beers were
placed in front of us.

"It's always good to relax after a long day," said Petr. "And I
wanted a chance to talk to you properly."

From the corner of my eye I noticed a door opening on a side
wall. Through it came a youth dressed only in a pair of white
underpants. For a second I thought it was Ivan and then I saw
the face was different. There was a smattering of applause as the
youth stepped onto a low-rise stage.

"You've heard about our serial killer, have you?" said Petr.

"What?" I said. And then, "Oh yes, I see." I clearly remembered the fat man on the plane although that seemed a while ago
now. "He cuts off their penises, doesn't he?"

On the stage the youth was gyrating his hips. Someone passed
him a bottle of oil or something and he held it vertically, squirted
the liquid on his chest. It made the already taut muscles glisten,
even in the half-light.

"It's our Catholic heritage," said Petr. "Where you have
rituals, you also have a perversion of them. That was one of the
plus points of communism. It didn't stand for all that. You knew
where you were with communism."

A barman appeared and replaced our two empty glasses
with two full ones. It was odd as I couldn't remember taking a

drink. The youth beckoned someone onto the stage with him, a muscular compact man from a table near the entrance.

The youth pushed the man to his knees in front of him and carefully took off his own underpants, revealing a large penis that was quickly growing erect. The man took the oil from the youth and started to rub it into the shaft of the penis, performing a slow masturbation.

"I wanted to bring you here," said Petr, "away from the hurly-burly, to explain the true nature of our task force. Can you keep a secret?"

"I'm sorry?"

"I wouldn't want this getting back to the captain."

"I keep myself to myself," I said.

The youth was sliding his hips slowly backward and forward, his penis slipping and sliding out of the O the man had made with his hand. On his face was a look of ecstasy.

"The main reason our bicycle task force has been set up is to catch this serial killer. Traditional methods have failed. The powers that be want to try something new. Are you willing to help?"

The muscular man, while keeping one hand in a perfect O, reached into a pocket and pulled out a small circular cracker. He held this near to the head of the penis. The youth gave one final thrust and came, the cum splashing onto the cracker. There was a loud round of applause and Petr asked me to repeat what I had said, my words obviously having been drowned out in the din.

"But why me?" I said again.

I couldn't remember the drive back to Petr's apartment. Our initial two beers had turned into seven or eight and the effect of the alcohol had only been intensified by my extreme tiredness.

The lift smelt of stale urine. Petr's door was at the end of a long corridor. I had the sense that we were very high up.

"Before we go in," said Petr, leaning close and whispering, "I must warn you of the mess. You understand, it has been a hectic few months, and certain things have slipped."

The apartment was one room divided down the center by a breakfast bar. There was one other door; a bathroom I assumed. As a place to live it was economical, neatly packaged. In the corner was a bed, unmade, blankets and sheets half on the floor. And across the floor were a series of Polaroid photos, all boys' faces.

"It's nothing like that," said Petr, who must have noticed the direction of my gaze. "My intentions are always toward females. These pictures, they are the victims." And then quite needlessly he added, "Of the serial killer."

Somehow, not wanting to get into all that now, it seeming a better topic for sobriety and the morning, I picked up the only other object on the floor. This was a wooden toilet seat fitted with four six-inch legs. I thought it perhaps an object of communism little talked about in the West.

"Ah that," said Petr. "That is my own design." He seemed flustered, his bluffness for the first time deteriorating. "You have to remember that with the end of communism came this sense that we could try almost anything, that anything was permissible in the market of supply and demand."

I turned the toilet seat over. Obviously, a lot of work had gone into it. Each of the legs fitted flush with the base and at the end of each leg was a perfect little wheel. I could imagine it scooting across the floor, almost a child's plaything.

"There is a certain lady I pay to lie below this seat," said Petr. "I like her there while I am watching the television. The sensation, how shall we say it, pleases me."

"I see," I said.

"At the time I am quite naked," said Petr. "It is only a little thing. Now," Petr clasped his hands together, "could I get you a nightcap?"

There was none of the usual awkwardness that comes when two men share a room, of working out who was going to sleep where. After all, there was only one bed. At some point Petr stood up and removed all his clothes. Due the smallness of the apartment I suddenly found myself face to face with Petr's extremely large and heavy penis. It was surrounded by a thick bush of hair. In fact, this hair continued all the way up Petr's body. My initial instinct was to reach out and cup the balls with my hand, but Petr currently being my immediate supervisor, I decided this was not a matter for consideration.

While Petr was in the toilet I removed my own clothes, rearranged the bed covers and slipped inside. I could clearly hear Petr grunting over the toilet bowl and I thought of that poor girl who was made to lie for hours with her face pressed against his arse. Or maybe not so poor, for who are we to judge others? Maybe this was her darkest wish too. Perhaps, in a Catholic sense, she saw Petr as her saint.

I must have been asleep when Petr got into bed for I don't remember him doing so. I woke up once and his arm was around me, his hairy front pressed to my smooth back. He had a night-time erection and his penis had worked its way so it was nestled between my thighs. The sensation was not unpleasant.

When I woke a second time light from a full moon was shining through the uncurtained window. In its spidery glow I could see picked out each of the faces of the murdered boys and every time I opened my eyes after this, feeling disconcerted, there they were. Eventually I could stand it no more and I got out from under the warmth of the bed and one by one turned them over to face the floor.

In my absence Petr had turned to the wall and the covers had slipped away. His arse was meaty, as hairy as his front. I got in next to him, nestled my own penis against this hairy area and fell back into a more than comfortable sleep.

I was dreaming of a steady life in Poland, with my own apartment, and myself as head of a bicycle task force when I felt myself being jolted awake. I opened my eyes to find Petr standing over me, still naked, phone pressed to his ear.

"It's Ivan," said Petr, and it took me a moment to comprehend he was speaking to me and not into the headset. "He's gone. They think the serial killer has struck again. Come, get ready. We must leave now."

I looked around the apartment for last night's discarded underpants. As I pulled them on over my morning erection I wondered what the day held in store for me.

The lads were in a state of high agitation. Apparently there had been an argument; teasing about the phallus had turned somewhat nasty and Ivan had said he was going home to his mother's.

"But that is strictly forbidden," said Petr.

Ivan's closest ally in the group, Stepanek, said he knew this, so he had contacted the mother in the early hours of the morning so that Ivan could return before his absence was noted. He was informed that Ivan had indeed been home but had only been there a few moments, in his own bedroom, before he had stormed out again with the words, "I will show those buggers. I will get the bastard myself."

Apparently unbeknownst to everyone but Stepanek, Ivan had been doing his own investigation into the serial killer and had confided to his friend that he had a more than firm lead.

"Then this morning," said Stepanek, "came the light."

I looked across at Petr and incomprehension must have shown on my face.

"There are certain details," said Petr, "in any investigation that are never released to the press. Just before dawn on the night of each killing, a light in the shape of a penis is shone into the sky. It is an indication of a murder."

Stepanek was almost beside himself. "Ivan is missing. It doesn't take a genius to work out the facts."

"You never know, until you know," said Petr. "Stepanek, we will go to his house. That is where the trail currently goes dead." At the door Petr turned and looked directly at me. "You too. You are needed. Your experience may help us dearly."

Ivan's mother was a tiny lady in a thick coat. She was far removed from the fine specimen that was Ivan. I was made to sit with her while Petr and Stepanek searched his room for clues. She served me a strong alcoholic drink in a tiny glass and passed me a plate of pickles to eat. I felt she was holding back, that at the slightest hint from me, she would burst into hysterical tears.

After what seemed like hours Petr and Stepanek emerged from the room. I could tell from their downcast faces that nothing had been found.

"If you don't mind..." I said.

Petr shook his head. "An extra pair of eyes. You may see what we did not."

The room had the unadorned transience of a room in an assignation house. Above the bed was a picture of a lake with ducks, in a corner a sparsely stacked bookcase, pornographic magazines spread across the bottom shelf. All these items, I imagined, had been duly noted and checked. No doubt Petr had not risen to his position of power by being unmethodical.

I remembered the way Ivan had looked at me as I applied the

lube to his arsehole, the mumbled "thank you." There had been a connection between us. Perhaps that's what Petr and Stepanek were missing, that connection.

Ivan had been bullied by the other boys and the nature of this bullying was over the phallus inside him. This was his sense of shame, not perhaps the object itself, but the others' perception of it. In the corner was a small wicker basket, an item that with no stretch of the imagination could be linked to laundry.

A large object up the arse may cause some bleeding and this blood in Ivan's mind would be symbolic of his humiliation. I guessed he would want to remove the pants that held this symbol.

Bingo! There, at the bottom, were the pants. I picked them up, and following my instinct, I held the front of the pants to my nose. The smell was masculine, comforting and intimate at the same time.

It was as I was placing the pants back that I noticed the slip of paper, lying alone at the bottom of the laundry basket. Its story was very short. *St. Barnabas Church,* it said.

"If I pushed Ivan the hardest," said Petr, "it was only because I felt he had the most exceptional talent."

Stepanek was sitting tight-lipped in the front of the car. I was squeezed in the back. We were worming our way upward, thick trees pressing in on either side.

Snow had started to fall again and when the trees did finally break I felt I had been presented with a scene you normally see in a snow globe.

The church stood alone on an outcropping of rock. Across its façade were flying buttresses, the carved faces of screaming monkeys, and below them, window after window after window, the glass a blaze of every color under the sun.

Access to the church was by a wooden walkway held secure by ropes above the precipice below. Petr went first, then Stepanek, then me. Once across, Petr held two fingers to his lips and gestured we should go to the side of the church.

"Who knows what we are getting ourselves into," he whispered.

About a third of the way down, at about knee height, was a small glass window.

"There is talk of St. Barnabas," said Stepanek, "that once you join its order you are there for life."

On the other side of the window was a room. It was sparsely lit, bare except for a stone table in the center. A door in the room opened and a young man stepped in. He was wearing a monk's habit and the back of his head was shaved in a perfect semicircle. He walked up to the table, lay his hands upon it, bent and kissed it reverently.

There was an air of serenity about the young man. He raised his hands to his neck and fumbled there and the habit fell away. He was naked underneath, his body perfectly shaved. He lifted himself up and lay facedown on the table, his legs slightly apart. Just visible was the tip of his penis, flattened against the tabletop.

The door of the room opened again and another young man entered. He was swinging a censer in front of him and by the way his lips were moving it was obvious he was reciting some incantation.

I was so drawn to the naked youth that I almost missed the third. This one had an extremely large nose and was holding a red cushion on the palm of his hand. In the center of this cushion was a small round wafer.

The youth on the table lifted his head slightly, looked around, smiled. The large-nosed youth placed the cushion down on the table, picked the wafer from it and very carefully parted the arsecheeks of the naked youth. The sphincter, like the rest of the body, was perfectly shaved.

"It's a kind of ceremony," whispered Stepanek.

I felt my own penis stiffen. In my head was Ivan. Unconsciously I had replaced the youth on the table with him.

The youth with the large nose bent forward, licked the arsehole with an almost feverish passion, so that when he came away the arsehole was glistening, even in the half-light. With his other hand he then pressed the wafer against the sphincter. After some initial resistance it disappeared inside and I could imagine it there and I wanted to be part of it. However, I was torn from my reverie by several things happening very quickly and almost at once.

Ivan stepped into the room, Stepanek called out his name, and Petr, Stepanek and I all felt the heavy fall of a hand on our shoulders. We leapt up and turned around and there were four more monks. Each was holding a gun. The guns were pointing at us.

We were standing before the priest. He was flanked on either side by the monks. A little away from them was Ivan, his head down.

"You do realize," said the priest, "that the interruption of the Eucharist is a very serious matter."

Petr's face flushed red. He stepped forward with clenched fists. The priest held up a hand.

"My son, your anger is best directed toward more productive avenues."

It was then Stepanek who spoke, voicing something that I myself had been thinking. "But Ivan, you are alive?"

Ivan looked puzzled. "Alive, but of course I am."

"We saw the light," said Stepanek. "We thought you were the next victim."

"Ah," said the priest, "that I can explain."

The priest led us back outside, back across the narrow wooden walkway. As we went he talked.

"The Church has its own way of dealing with these serial killers. A trap was laid. A monk was set as bait. The serial killer struck."

"The monk was killed?" I said.

"Oh no," said the priest. He stopped. We were in a barren field a short distance from the church. "The monk was saved but the killer escaped. He left only this." The priest pointed toward a contraption on the ground. It was a light box.

"The penis in the sky," said Petr.

"The net is closing," said the priest. He turned to Ivan. "And you, my boy, must make your choice. It is the bicycle task force or my monks. The State or the Church. In Poland that is the way it has always been."

Ivan put a hand up to his mouth then dropped it. He looked at me. "What about you," he said. "What are you going to do?"

Petr pursed his lips. "I can swing it with your captain. Say you are doing important work here. It's your choice."

My choice, I thought and then again, *Why me?* This time though, there was a competing and more appealing thought. *Why not?*

I was assigned a room in the barracks with Ivan. By day I was advisor to the bicycle task force, by night I slept side by side with Ivan. On our third night together he slipped his penis inside me. There was no ceremony about it and no talk. I liked the feel of it there and pushed myself back against him. As he came he twisted my head around and kissed me.

"Do you believe in love at first sight?" he said.

I thought of my life up until then, my life in the barracks back home. I had been an outsider, excluded. There had been no room for love. Everything had been a series of feints, moves, ritual maneuvering.

"Can I fuck you?" I said.

Ivan gripped my arsecheeks as I fucked him, his legs over my shoulders. It was my first time and I watched the head of my penis as it disappeared inside him. After, we showered together. Ivan got down on his knees and took each of my balls in his mouth. As we were getting dried Ivan passed me his underpants.

"Would you wear these today? I want to think of you in them."

Then we were back outside. Petr arrived later than usual and he asked to speak to me in private. He was holding a slip of paper.

"It's bad news," he said. "The killer has struck again. This time for real. They want us to go fully operational, now rather than later. Do you think you're ready?"

I was aching where Ivan had been inside me. I thought of more nights of us inside each other. Somehow this felt like the important thing. Everything else was peripheral, even death.

"Let's go for it," I said.

BURNING THE MIDNIGHT OIL

Michael Cain

Andy stumbled through my dorm room door. A thin sheen of sweat showed on his forehead and moistened his bulging biceps and forearms. His light blond hair was matted—and he was missing a sock.

"Where have you been? Project's due on Monday," I said, sitting at my desk, and getting a woody looking at him. Six feet tall; a tight, sweet body; the bluest eyes.

"It was only twenty minutes," he countered, raking a hand through his disheveled locks.

So he had timed this break? I had an idea why.

"So what were ya doing?" I said in my best sorority-girl chirp.

"Shane...er—he needed me."

"Needed you, how?" I couldn't contain my curiosity. And thank god I had a book in my lap, or I wouldn't have been able to contain my erection either.

"You know...boyfriend stuff."

I raised my eyebrows.

"He needed to fuck me before he went to sleep."

Bingo!

"I thought jocks were supposed to abstain before a big game," I said.

"Well, yeah. But we broke that rule once, and they won against a top-ten team. So now it's before every game."

"Charming..." I adjusted my erection. "But you don't look like a man who just got off."

"What's that supposed to mean?"

Ah, I'd hit a nerve. "Nothing, really. Just...most guys look... relaxed and, well...happy after they shoot."

He scratched the back of his neck in consternation.

"Shane's under a lot of pressure. I don't expect him to expend the extra...energy to get me off."

I gave him an *Oh, that's so pitiful* roll of my eyes. He slumped against the edge of my desk, right where I wanted him.

"I'll take care of it later," he said.

By now his cock was as hard as mine, bulging under his jeans. I reached out, grabbing him by the waistband, and pulled him to me. From eye level with his crotch, I looked up into his pretty-boy face.

"I think I can help with that," I said.

He gulped, troubled by the push and pull between doing the right thing thing, and need.

But I didn't hear *no, don't,* or *I can't.*

What I heard was him breathing heavily as I deftly undid his jeans, pulling them open and scooping out his swollen cock and balls. What I felt was the softness of his skin, the hardness of his generously endowed dick in my hand, and the grip of his hands on my shoulders. What I tasted was sweet sweat and salty precome.

Yeah, he really needed to shoot his load!

His breath caught with a hiss as I took him in my mouth, swirling my tongue, swallowing him whole. I'm a saxophone player, a pretty good one—classical, jazz, whatever—so I have a talented mouth. I could've made Andy blow his load in thirty seconds, if I had wanted to. But the monster between my legs was hungry for his ass, and I always do right by my monster.

So I teased and sucked, and then I stopped. I teased, I sucked, gave it a lick, stopped again. After about five agonizing minutes Andy's legs were shaking and his fingers were laced around the back of my head, messing up my hair.

I didn't mind.

I was going to mess up more than just his hair!

I spat his cock out of my mouth and gazed up with faux concern.

"What's wrong? Why aren't you coming?"

"I...I..." he said, breathing like he'd run a marathon, more sweat seeping through his T-shirt, plastering it to his powerful torso. Andy was on the swim team: everything about him was toned, if not bulging, under his creamy, lightly tanned flesh.

I stood up and helpfully tugged his soaked shirt over his head, tossing it on the floor, exposing his smooth, heaving chest and broad shoulders.

"N-nothing...nothing's wrong." He coughed and his seven-inch cock bounced enticingly. "I just—usually I can't come unless...you know...?"

Indeed I did.

"Unless what, Andy?"

He shook his head.

"Unless Shane's fucking me." He sounded both embarrassed and breathlessly horny.

"Oh?" I furrowed my brow again and then smiled brightly,

an *I've got a great idea* smile. I reached into my pocket and produced a purple-foiled condom.

"I don't know…" he said, looking commendably torn.

"Yeah, I know," I said, dropping the rubber on my desk. From my other pocket I pulled out a Trojan Magnum and handed it to him. He started to shake his head, but then stopped, registering the contents of the foil package.

I ripped my polo shirt off, noting how Andy's eyes shone as he took in my body; I don't have a football player's physique, but Andy wasn't the only one on the swim team.

Then I played my ace.

I pulled open my pants, unzipped my fly, and let my monster burst free. He never needs an invitation, just a way out: a downward-pushed zipper, fretfully worn trouser material…

Andy's mouth fell open. I was tempted to push him down on his knees, to coax him into giving me a blow job, but my monster wanted the entree, not an appetizer!

He looked from my pulsing cock to my eyes and then back to my cock. More troublesome contemplation. "I really shouldn't…"

Shouldn't! Not can't. *Can't* and I might have backed off. But he just said *shouldn't*.

"Shhhh," I breathed, pressing two fingers against his pretty lips. He started to open his mouth, so I put my talented lips to good use again, pulling him to me, kissing him with the passion of one thousand and one hard-ons.

He submitted, and, god, he tasted good!

I gently pushed him away—only to arm's length—then squeezed his hand holding the Trojan Magnum. "What are you waiting for? Roll it on me."

He fumbled with the packet for a moment, then resorted to tearing it open with his teeth. The condom fit snugly. I reached around and cupped each orb of his ass with my hands and lifted him onto my desk, playfully kissing and nipping at the flesh of his neck with my lips and teeth. He fell back at the lightest of pushes, and I made fast work of his clinging jeans and tennis shoes.

I left the one sock on for effect.

His hole winked at me right before I pushed into him. His sphincter may have been fucked not minutes before, but he hissed with painful pleasure as my cock stretched his anus and I poked around in his warm center.

"Oh, man! You're too big!" His cheeks blushed and his ass squirmed, trying to expel my cock. But my monster was inside and wasn't going anywhere. I pushed down on his chest with one hand and found his stone-hard dick with the other. I leaned in and spat saliva on his cock, slathering it with my fist, then I pulled halfway out and slammed right back in, to the fucking hilt.

I pushed and pulled myself in and out of him, pumping his cock with my fist, giving him the royal treatment.

Suddenly his hand latched onto my spit-slicked fist.

"Stop!" he panted. "Don't wanna come yet..." he said, in a breathless heave.

So I paused briefly, then I let go of his cock, crawled up on the desk, folded Andy's hot body in half, and started power-fucking his ass like a goddamn locomotive, making the milky white flesh of his ass jounce with every plunge of my prick into his hole.

Objects were falling off my desk and onto the tile floor, both of us were cursing, pleading for more—*harder! tighter! faster!*—and a slapping, suction-cup sort of sound was increasing in volume.

Andy looked into my eyes—the look of disbelief, mingled with ardent lust, told me my plan had succeeded. With my cock jackhammering his ass, I was ruining him for all other men. Even his beautiful boyfriend, what's-his-name, the quarterback! I came up Andy's very well-fucked ass, swelling the Trojan Magnum to the brink. Andy came in concert with my hardest, most fervent thrusts, splattering my chest, his cheek, and the tilted screen of my laptop with copious jets of spunk.

I pulled out, sauntered to the bathroom to dispose of the jizz-filled condom, and took a well-deserved piss.

Lust was unmistakably etched across his face when I returned. I threw him a towel and then handed him his clothes. He looked confused.

"I thought we could...you know, go again?"

I smiled. Lit a cigarette.

"Nah. You go home, get a good night's sleep, and come back tomorrow night."

I slapped his bare ass as I scooted him stark naked out the door. "I want you fresh next time—all mine."

FLUID MECHANICS

Dale Chase

Nobody knows because nobody looks, not a bad thing so long as you alter perspective to embrace obscurity. I can cross the entire university campus with no more than the occasional nod or "Hello, Professor Blaine." I return the greeting in kind even as the anarchist who's recently taken up residence inside me urges me to fuck them all.

It's a savory sort of conundrum and I move about toting it as one would an untimely erection, enjoying the fullness while not as yet getting it out, so to speak. I lecture and tutor and consult, interacting with students and faculty while beset by this new arousal and yet at night, when logic says I could get it out and have my way, I sleep as never before.

I don't question why the anarchist has sprouted within me, I simply enjoy his presence, relishing the need he thus far has displayed only to me. It's possession of the highest order, dick within a dick, and I wait to see what he'll do.

Of course I will at some point fuck. Years of restraint will ultimately give way and it won't be some bathroom quickie or lengthy courting ritual over expensive meals. No, it will be lust unleashed, Father Nature baring all to obliterate the empty decorum on which life is needlessly built. The worst fuck, the best fuck, nasty and uplifting at once, soaring cock trailing excrement-tinged come. I shall open a bottom and climb in, Alice down the rabbit hole. I shall smother myself as I come and come and come.

My first outward—to me—concession is to stop wearing underwear. Nobody knows as I move about with just khaki between my anxious cock and the students. I become erect behind the lectern and pride myself on my ability to detail fluid mechanics without pause while fighting the urge to bare my dick. I pontificate about the Navier-Stokes equations, discussing velocity and pressure in the flow of fluids, and as I hear myself speak, the anarchist looks out at the comatose throng and thinks of the only fluid that matters in life. He urges me to step from behind the lectern, get out my dick and wake them with a demonstration. He wants my spunk shooting at them, my hand guiding an endless spray, pumping and pumping, breaking the laws of physics, ethics, and humanity itself. The anarchist thrills to the duplicity yet he allows the professor to lose neither his decorum nor his job while the students remain unenlightened.

When the sex does happen it is, oddly, not my doing. A student, Jeremy, quite gifted and one of many I enjoy gazing upon, knocks on my office door one Tuesday and rushes in, apologizing for not making an appointment. Clearly distraught, he tells me his life has collapsed. His parents are divorcing and funding for his education is suspended. As he crashes about the room wailing that his life will end with the semester, it hits me: *My god, I'm going to fuck him.*

I wait for a break in his lament to offer alternative funding sources and a good dose of encouragement but the anarchist in me has climbed atop the pillars and bared his cock. I watch Jeremy, twenty-year-old physics major, brilliant, blond, slight, tousled, and I uncross my legs, allow a hand to slide into my lap where I prod my swollen prick. God, let me get it out and solve his problems. But then Jeremy has run down, slumped into the chair opposite, and now looks at me. "What can I do?"

He knows the answer as well as I. No student is ignorant of loans and scholarships and the practicalities of life so I view his question as one of personal need. He is hurt by thoughts of abandonment, frightened at the consequences. He doesn't want practical advice, he wants comfort.

"You can do what a great many students do," I tell him. "Apply for loans, scholarships. Take a part-time job if necessary. I worked my way through college and there's actually a great sense of accomplishment in paying your own way." *Now take down your pants and come sit on my dick*, the anarchist cries. He laughs at teacher's claptrap. *Fuck is the answer. Bend him over. Put it in.*

Jeremy looks away because he doesn't want advice. He wants an ally and I find myself flattered that he might think it me. A surge of compassion rushes forth. I want to hold him, care for him, reassure him. *Let me suck your dick.*

I retain my composure because that's what I do, although I do it seated due to my erection. Jeremy gradually calms and accepts that he will be on his own and I find hope in him trying to embrace independence. *He has no ties. I will fuck him.*

Twenty years lie between us but it is that difference that matters most. The wisdom of experience is the gift I can offer, that and my cock. "When the semester ends you can move to my guest room if you like. By then you'll have a feel for how you're going to handle things."

"You'd take me in?"

"Of course. You're one of my best students. It would be a great loss if you left us." *Left me*, the anarchist cries.

Tears come to Jeremy's eyes, such is his relief. He smiles and in doing this, catches my eye. I hold his gaze long enough for him to understand that something is beginning between us. He does not flee. Rather, he quiets and I see consideration run through him. It's a glorious moment, the birth of possibility, and I am content when he rises to leave. "Thank you, Professor Blaine."

"You're quite welcome."

When I'm alone I lock my door and get out my cock and my handkerchief. I sit in my chair and work myself, thinking of Jeremy naked in my guest room. I see myself standing in the doorway with my cock pointed at him. He raises his legs, shows me where he wants it, and I climb onto the bed and shove it into his pristine ass and we fuck and fuck and fuck and I come and come and come.

When I'm done with the real thing I wipe away my cream and sigh with contentment but the anarchist does not join me. I put away my cock but he insists I look at the calendar, add up the days until semester's end.

There are just eighteen, which I remind myself is a small number. Until then I live on anticipation, calling on Jeremy in class and counseling him afterward. Life is suddenly beautiful because we will fuck.

When he moves his meager belongings into the room in December I want to do it then and there as the anarchist screams to set down the bags and fuck. I don't try to hide my erection and Jeremy glances down, smiling shyly, which makes me want it all the more but I don't press, not just yet. And then he's telling me he won't go home for Christmas due to the unrest so I invite him to celebrate with me, knowing by then we'll be at it like rabbits.

He is neat and clean. We share a bathroom and I encounter him in the hall in just a towel. His hair is wet, curls at the neck, and we stand immobile. "I hope I didn't use all the hot water," he says somewhat sheepishly. So polite. *Let me lick your bottom.*

I cannot sleep with him in the house. Our first night is spent with him undoubtedly snoring away and me frantically abusing myself. I spray come; I shove a dildo up my ass; I work my cock until it's red.

I want to go down the hall and invade him, take him in his sleep if need be, just get into him. And I want his prick as well because penetration is a universal condition and everyone needs a rear assault now and again whether or not they'll admit it.

We chastely coexist for two days and then he calls his mother one evening, which is his undoing. I eavesdrop from the next room, hear it all. He is quiet, subdued, listening mostly, then sobbing by degrees and finally angry. There is no good-bye and I hear him slam down the phone.

When I join him he's pacing, flushed, tears all down his cheeks. "Come here," I say as I step into his path and he falls into my arms. His sobs resume, a veritable eruption. I hold him, head on my chest, tears wetting my shirt. My cock is up and pressed against him. I rub his back to quiet him and he gradually settles. It is then I begin.

I slide my hands onto his bottom and pull him to me. He's still agitated and it's this I draw upon. As I rub against him, I feel his cock awaken. "You need to get past them," I say. "You must take charge of yourself, see to your own needs. Your life doesn't have to fall apart because of them."

I squeeze his bottom as I say this, which causes him to wriggle in my grasp. "You know what you need," I say and I let go of his bottom to take down his zipper.

He doesn't resist. In fact, when I have his cock out he seems most anxious to shed his pants. I watch as he strips naked.

When he stands bare, holding a small but persistent prick, I feel a moment of anguish that anyone could hurt such an innocent creature but then I catch myself and attend to the matter at hand. I strip, then beckon him into my arms.

Clutching his body against my own causes him to come. I feel his spurts between us as he cries out and shudders and I wallow in our slippery connection.

His head is on my chest and I slip a hand to the back of it, push him to my tit where he takes hold and sucks frantically. As he feeds I tell him we must fuck.

I lead him to my bedroom where I arrange him on the bed. When I raise his legs he pulls them high, slides his arms around them to hold the position and I see he's experienced. His pink hole quivers and I realize he's clenching his muscle. As I apply the condom I wonder how many cocks he's had but when I run a gob of lube into him and feel his tightness I forget them all and embrace the moment. He's watching me now, holding his prick and waiting for mine.

When I'm in position I want to tell him what this is for me, how my dick in his bottom is bliss, ecstasy, nirvana, but I know not to say such things because it's not the professor who'll fuck, it's the anarchist and we are just beginning.

As I push in and experience his spongy warmth, a jolt slices through me from balls to spine and back again and this causes a small shout to escape me but then I'm off on a rampage, thrusting madly as I look at his pink tits and his prick, which is spraying come again. The sight of his hand pulling at it inflames me and I think of eating the morsel and wish I could feed and fuck at the same time.

I look down at our connection, watch my cock go up him over

and over and this fixation brings on a climax. As it beckons I grow frantic, ramming it home, and then I am unleashed. Professor, anarchist, prick—no matter, it's a come, a come, a come.

When at last I'm empty an anguish overtakes me, not unfamiliar but not welcome either, and I pull out, toss the rubber, then get my mouth down where no mouth belongs and lick the residue and put in my tongue, still fucking. He grabs his cock.

I'm like a pig at a trough, snuffling and snorting. I keep at him until my jaw starts to ache and only then relent but when I sit back and see the whole of him, so pink and fresh, I want to dirty him so I fall onto him, flatten him under me and drive my just-up-his-rectum tongue into his mouth. To my surprise he not only takes it, he sucks it, which is the closest you can get to eating your own ass.

I writhe atop him and he finds my spent dick and pulls at it, which is futile at the moment yet still pleasurable. And then I pull off him, see his mouth still open like some hungry baby bird's and it drives me mad so I crawl up onto him, stuff my limp dick into it. He takes hold, sucks like he's starving, and as he does this I manage a rather masterful, near-acrobatic reversal so I can gobble his dick while mine remains inside his eager mouth and thus I suck him as he sucks me, feasting until he rewards me with a few more spurts.

He is still sucking my cock when I decide we're done and as I pull out I hear his tongue still working, still sucking. I reverse, slide up next to him, quiet him. "Enough," I whisper as I pull him into my arms. "Sleep now." He quiets and in seconds I hear his soft snore.

Lying with him I remind myself of just what I have here, hoping satisfaction will lull me toward sleep, but the anarchist glances at the clock to calculate the next fuck at dawn. Turns out he's wrong because I awaken in the night, emerge hard from vague dreams, and I find Jeremy's bottom and shove a finger up him.

He awakens enough to respond, pushes his ass back at me to encourage the prodding and I add a second digit, working my dick with my other hand. If I fuck now, I may be ready again before morning classes.

The covers are thrown off, he's still riding my fingers, and with my free hand I grab a condom from the nightstand. I pull out of him only to suit up and lube, then I pull his ass high and push in.

"I'm going to fuck you raw," I growl in a voice not my own. I ram it in for emphasis and he clutches the sheet. *Fuck, fuck, fuck*—a mantra now, anarchist loose in the night. *Fuck him*, he prods. *Fuck his sweet ass, get it up there, fuck, fuck, fuck.* He keeps at it like he's riding me and I see us now as a threesome, dick up my own ass, which seems at the moment entirely possible. Grunting and sweating, reduced to filthy animal, at last comes the rise and I claw at flesh, pounding and pumping as it shoots out of me. Pain sears my chest, I cannot breathe, I may die fucking but don't care because I'm giving it to him, filling his ass with spunk. I hear "Fuck, fuck, fuck" as I spurt and shudder and when I run dry I keep at it because I want to fuck forever or die trying. My cock allows a few seconds of such indulgence before succumbing to reality. I slide out and fall onto my back.

In the dark, as I gasp for air, I feel Jeremy's cock against my leg and hear his urgent whisper. "Let me fuck you," he rasps and when I offer no response because the anarchist is momentarily stunned and the professor is near death, he crawls over me, gets a rubber, applies it. My hand reaches for the lamp, turns it on because I want to see him like this. His teeth are bared, jaw clenched; he's like a lion cub who's just found his dick. I lie back, raise my legs and show him my hole. His mouth falls open, he licks his lower lip as he guides his prick into me. *"Fuck you,"* says the anarchist.

How can anyone on earth forswear the joy of penetration? As the persistent cock thrusts in short quick strokes, I am transported to ass-tingling heaven and I hitch my legs higher and clench my muscle, trying to suck his dick as he fucks me. And when he comes, which is all too soon, he is as frantic with his words as his cock. "I'm there, oh shit, I'm there, I'm there," as if I couldn't tell he's shooting come up my butt.

He fucks with a stamina I envy, going on even after his exclamations have stopped, and when he finally relents and pulls out I lower my legs and leap onto him, pull off the rubber and get my mouth on his prick, tasting the come, sucking him and handling his balls as if I can squeeze out still more. He lies quiet as I go at him and it is the quiet that ultimately stops it. I hear myself, alone now, sucking dick when it's over. I fall back, fall over, fall asleep.

He's gone when I awaken to my alarm at seven. I leap up, rush to his room, find him absent. For a second I'm in complete panic as I fear he's fled the nest but then I see it's just his neatness. His handful of CDs are stacked on the desk, his clothes hang in the closet. An early class, then, and this knowledge gets me into my day. In the shower as I soap my dick I think of the night, know it was real even though there is a dreamlike quality. I run a finger up my crack, feel my pucker, push in. Yes.

In the lecture hall that afternoon I see Jeremy fourth row center. My dick gets hard and the anarchist reminds me it's a new day. As I launch into fluid mechanics, detailing the properties of random turbulence, the anarchist has a good laugh.

TALKING TO MR. MACK

Thomas Fuchs

Mr. Mack kept his apartment dark and sat with his back to the one window that didn't have a shade so, particularly on a bright day like this, you couldn't see his face very well and there was no way to tell what he was thinking. Sammy wondered if that was deliberate, a way to get power over him. Mr. Mack was such a drama queen. The way he just buzzed you in without a word and then left his door half open and in you came and it was like you were onstage, kind of, a stage where Mr. Mack had the first line, which was, "What have you brought me?"

"I fucked this guy down," said Sammy. "Not what he came for but that's what he got."

"That's a good setup," said Mr. Mack. "What did he come for?"

"Massage."

"You got him from Craigslist?"

"He found me, answered my post. Not Craigslist. Massage-Boyz, I think."

"How many lists are you on?"

"Too many, and some chatrooms, but I have to make money."

"So did he come to your place?"

"Yep."

"What did he look like?"

"Cute, actually. Surfer build. Not too old and in good shape. Rugged face."

"Surfer blond?"

"Sorta brown. He said he's straight, girlfriend out of town."

"A story we've heard before."

Sammy nodded and smiled. He was a nice-looking kid: early twenties, curly black hair, olive skin. Dark eyes. Not Latin, more Mediterranean. Mr. Mack thought he looked a little like Sal Mineo. Sammy wouldn't have any idea who Sal was—very different generations.

"So, surfer bod? Smooth?"

"Yeah, pretty smooth. Nice chest hair, not too thick. Kind of silky. And you know what, he wasn't shaved but he was trimmed, which straight guys don't usually do."

"No, they don't. You said he was in shape but old. How old?"

Sammy shrugged. "Rugged look. Maybe late thirties. But great definition."

"So he came up to your place? Was it spur of the moment or did he have an appointment?"

"Spur of the moment."

"Do you find those are the guys who want more than a massage, when they need it right away?"

Sammy smiled. "They all want more than just a massage. Mostly. I have had a few guys say no hand job, just a massage, but mostly they expect it."

"Particularly when they tell you the girlfriend's out of town."

"Yep."

"Did you start him on his stomach or his back?"

So many questions, thought Sammy. In a way, Mr. Mack was the weirdest of his clients, and the most exhausting.

"On his stomach or his back?" asked Mr. Mack again.

"His stomach. Gave him the Sammy Special on his shoulders, his neck. Used a little oil. Cracked his back."

"Any incense?"

"No. Just oil."

"What kind of oil, Sammy? Details. You know I need details."

"Uh...massage oil."

"Aromatic?"

Sammy thought hard. What was that oil called? "Uh, sandalwood." He wasn't sure it really was sandalwood but the answer satisfied Mr. Mack, who nodded and said, "Okay, go on. You cracked his back, and then?"

"He had a real nice ass."

"Tell me about it. Was it smooth, his ass?" Mr. Mack leaned forward as he said this and it seemed to Sammy that he was breathing a little faster, but he was still sitting behind his desk, so Sammy couldn't tell for sure if he was getting excited.

"Pretty smooth," said Sammy. "Not shaved but not much hair. Nice ass. Hard."

"Bubble butt?"

"No, not really. But nice shape. Nice legs. Big."

"You wouldn't mind fucking him?"

"Well, I didn't think about it, I guess. I just started getting hard."

"And then...?"

"Uh," said Sammy, "so I, you know, ran my finger up the back of his balls and along his crack and he wriggled around a little and he made these sounds."

"Sounds? What kind of sounds?"

"*Ohhh...*" said Sammy, drawing out the word, and then, "*Ah...ohhh*" and did such a bad job of it that the moan became a giggle. "I can't do it the way he did. I'm not an actor."

"That's okay," said Mr. Mack. "You're doing fine. So he was spreading his legs and letting you know what he wanted."

"Yeah. Uh, no, not for sure. But I was thinking probably."

"He didn't actually say, fuck me, or anything?"

"No."

"Maybe he was on the edge about it. Didn't want to say he wanted it."

Sammy nodded.

"Didn't even admit to himself that's what he wanted," said Mr. Mack.

"Could be," said Sammy, and thought that his head was going to explode. Could they just get on with what happened?

Mr. Mack prompted him. "He was on his stomach and...?"

"I flipped him over, did his front."

"You didn't want to fuck him when he was on his stomach?"

"He came for a massage so he got a massage. That's what he paid for."

"You said he came for more."

"I meant a hand job. They expect that usually."

"But they don't expect to get fucked?"

"Not the massage clients, usually. For one thing, that's a different rate and sometimes we discuss that after the massage, if they came for a massage but then that's what they want."

"What about the hand job?"

"That's part of the massage."

"Okay, so let's not race ahead. About the hand job...nice dick? Tell me about it."

"About this big around," said Sammy, making a circle with his thumb and forefinger, big enough that he didn't close the circle. "And about, um, seven inches."

"And you worked over every inch of it?"

"Just teased it, got it nice and perky. But he kept spreading his legs, you know?"

"Use your mouth on it?"

"Naw."

"Lube?"

"Oh, sure."

"But he didn't cum?"

"No, cause by then I was getting really interested in fucking him even if he wasn't gonna pay for it, so I stopped and then you know what I did?"

"What did you do?" The old man leaned forward slightly and turned his head and the light fell on his face and Sammy could see the lines and the sagging pouches under his eyes.

"Well, you know," said Sammy, "sometimes I can be bad."

"So you've told me."

"You like it when I'm bad, don't you?"

"Just give me the details, Sammy. That's what I like."

In fact, it was difficult for Sammy sometimes, remembering what his different clients liked. This was Sammy's third visit to Mr. Mack's, or was it his fourth, and he still hadn't quite got a handle on what the guy was looking for, what turned him on.

"You were saying you wanted to fuck him, even though he hadn't come for that, wasn't going to pay for that?"

"Completely right," said Sammy.

"So after the massage and working his dick...?"

"Uh, then I sat on his face."

"Really?"

"Well, you know, I sort of squatted and hung my dick down

onto his mouth."

"Kind of daring to do that to a straight guy," said Mr. Mack, "whose girlfriend was..." and he paused and Sammy joined in and in unison they said, "...out of town!" and laughed and then Mr. Mack continued with his questions. "Did he say anything when you stuck your dick in his face?"

"No. He didn't have to say anything, did he?"

"Sometimes they say *Wow* or something like that, you've told me."

"Yeah," said Sammy. He wasn't a big guy, five-foot-eight, one hundred forty-five, but he was well muscled and well hung. He liked thinking about the number of times guys had said *Wow*. He was getting hard. Telling Mr. Mack these stories wasn't so bad, really. Kind of fun, reliving what had happened.

"So, you had your dick down in front of his face..."

"Yeah. Well, he licked it and then I pushed a little bit, you know, and he opened wide, and I pushed it in and he was pretty good, kept his teeth out of the way but he didn't do too much, so I pushed in all the way and he started to gag, so I pulled it out real quick."

"And?"

"And then I got him to sit up and I stood over him and then I stuck it back in and told him to relax and I worked him like I told him I was gonna work his ass. I asked him was that what he wanted and he couldn't say anything because I was in him but I knew the answer because he started making more of an effort. He sucked when I pulled and I told him to use his tongue and he did but he really wasn't too good at cocksucking, I have to say, but he did get me nice and hard."

"See, you're not so bad at telling a story once you get going. Telling a story isn't that much different from a good fucking. You've got to get a rhythm going. So then after he got you hard, did you think you were going to cum?"

"Naw," said Sammy. "I got a little precum going, that's true, and he lapped that up, but I pulled out and I pushed him back down and you know I was really in control. Which is one of the things I like if the guy's bigger than me, which this guy was, did I tell you that? He turned over, back onto his stomach, that's the way he wanted it, so then I pushed him in the ass, you know, with my foot and told him to hike it up in the air and he did."

"You were in charge by then?"

"As usual," said Sammy, smiling.

"Then what happened?"

"I fucked him."

"Details."

Mr. Mack wanted so much! "My brain hurts," said Sammy.

"I know the feeling, believe me, but we must press on. Did you just shove your dick into him or was there more foreplay?"

"I put some lube on him, worked my finger in. He took it no trouble so then I used two and worked him around. He wasn't too loose, which is good you know."

"Yes, I know."

"But he was kinda dirty. Hadn't cleaned himself up nice."

"Ugh. I see. Evidence that he is not an experienced bottom."

"I'm pretty sure I was his first. For a long time anyway. So I put a rubber on my fingers. Then I gave him the vibrating fingers bit against his prostate. He really liked that, my surfer guy. Started twisting around and…" Sammy gasped, imitating the man's reaction. "He really liked that. Then you know what I did?"

"Tell me, Sammy."

"I flipped him over on his back 'cause I wanted to look at his face while I did him."

"Wait, wait. That's interesting. That's good. But don't go so fast. You flipped him over. How did you do that?"

"I have my ways."

"No, really. Details, Sammy."

"I stood up and I grabbed his ankles and I straightened out his legs and then I stepped over, twisted him from the hips. And he flipped right over."

"Kind of like wrestling."

"Control your man," said Sammy. "So then I pushed his legs back over, you know, got his ankles almost down to his ears. He was mine, all mine, wide open."

"Rape fantasy?"

Sammy grinned and shook his head. "Naw, he wanted it, didn't he, so it's not rape."

"Maybe he was playing out some fantasy," said Mr. Mack, "because he really does have a girlfriend and he was conflicted about wanting to get fucked so he had to pretend it was being forced on him."

Sammy shrugged. "Don't know. Could be."

"On the other hand," said Mr. Mack, "a manly man might not want to admit to being raped."

Sammy shrugged again.

Mr. Mack said, "It's hard to know what's on a person's mind sometimes, what they're thinking, what they really want and why they want it."

Sammy said nothing, waiting for this unremarkable train of thought to play itself out.

"Ah, well," said Mr. Mack, "I'll work on it later. Go on."

"Where was I?"

"You had him loosened up and on his back."

"Not too loose, but I'm telling you his hole was pulsing with pleasure by that point. I don't know if he wanted it, but his pussy sure did."

"Pulsing with pleasure? *Pulsating*, you mean. Pulsating with pleasure, I think."

"Whatever," said Sammy. "He was digging it. He was twitching all over the place and I really got into it."

"You were working that prostate."

"I was making it sing! At first he was in a little pain, I think. *Ow, ow*...but then he relaxed and I was playing his prostate like a stick on a drum and he was shouting every time I slammed into him, and I was slamming my whole body into him. And then I slowed it up and then I speeded it up and his face started to melt, you know."

"Melt?"

"You know. I can't explain it."

"Try. Details."

Sammy made a face, cocking his head to one side, dropping his jaw, rolling his eyes. Then he snapped back to normal, and grinned. "Like that," he said.

"I've never seen anyone go like that."

"You never fucked anyone like I do."

"Did his mouth really drop open like that?"

"Yeah and he was making that *ah-ah-ah* sound. And a couple of *oh gods*, I think."

"And his head was rolling around?"

"His whole body was bucking but yeah a couple of times it looked like his neck was broken and he stopped moving. And his eyes rolled back. He'd be like that and then it's like he got more strength and he started bucking around and growling and *ah ahh* and that. And then he started shooting, cum all over the place."

"And you pulled out?"

"Not right away."

"That wasn't polite."

"I wasn't a good host, I guess. But then I pulled out 'cause

I like to shoot 'em in the face. I told him to close his eyes and I
let loose. It was nice and thick and there was a lot of it. He was
a mess!"

"And then?"

"It was getting late. I had to go meet some friends. So I just
sorta grabbed him by the hair, you know, and sat him up. He
was pretty knocked out but I told him it was shower time. He
blew me in the shower, by the way. Just a little bit. Felt real
good."

"I should think so," said Mr. Mack.

"The water running down all around you and this guy on his
knees sucking you. Ummm."

"And that was it?"

"Well, I toweled him off. Rubbed him good. Made him feel
good."

"And then?"

"Then he left."

"No final words? You know how much I like final words."

"Yeah," Sammy strained to think. "Oh, yeah. I said thanks
for coming and he thought that was a joke, you know, *cumming*.
And the last thing he said was, 'Gee, I wasn't expecting that.'"

"That's pretty good," said Mr. Mack, "I like that—'I wasn't
expecting that.'"

"That's what he said," said Sammy.

Mr. Mack stood up. "Good report. Thank you." He handed
Sammy his sixty dollars and walked him to the door.

"I did okay?"

"You were great."

"I was thinking maybe I should keep a notebook or something."

Mr. Mack was startled by that, "No, no... Just tell me what
happens as best you can. As directly as you can. Just the way

we've been doing it." He laughed.

"What's funny?"

"I just suddenly had this image in my head of you straddling some guy, fucking him, then stopping and jotting something down on a pad, and then back to fucking him."

"Maybe I should videotape the whole thing, with a hidden camera," said Sammy.

"There wouldn't be any inner life to that," said Mr. Mack, taking him seriously. "That's a different kind of storytelling."

"Okay," said Sammy. Theory meant little to him. "Well, call me again when you want, okay?"

"You bet." As soon as Sammy was out the door, Mr. Mack sat back at his desk and turned on the computer, groping for an opening, a setting of the scene, physical and emotional, and then began writing: *Mr. Mack kept his apartment dark and sat with his back to the one window that didn't have a shade so, particularly on a bright day like this...* No, no point in taking that much time for the setup, move it along.... He picked another point in the story and began typing...stopped again and thought and began again: *My girlfriend was out of town, visiting her folks, so this was my chance. I'd seen this particular posting before and I was really curious to try what I'd been fantasizing about for a long time.* Mr. Mack settled in, spinning out the story as it came to him, reporting and inventing, imposing sense and form on sensation and desire.

THE KEY-MAKER'S WIFE

Ted Cornwell

"This truck's been through worse shit before, and there's more to come," Serge says after one particularly alarming pothole. Brian turns a sickly shade of pale. Serge jams Soul Asylum into the dashboard tape deck, but the sound is barely audible above the Precambrian roar of his pickup. Brian focuses on a clump of trees ahead, trying to quell his nausea.

Serge resumes his story. He's been explaining that he was named after a great-uncle, who had *not* been named Sergeant, but who'd risen to that rank in the army before perishing in Vietnam. So this is the derivation of Sergeant Ramos. Brian would have found it fascinating and alluring if only he weren't concentrating so hard on the effort not to barf. Ever since he was a child, Brian has suffered from motion sickness. Why he'd agreed to go hurtling down some redneck highway toward a fishing hole in the Chesapeake Bay now seems a great mystery to him. Baltimore recedes in the rearview mirror like a scolding aunt whose advice should have been heeded.

Serge continues. His mother now thinks the name is a curse. She worries that with the war in Iraq, the government will start a draft again, and Serge will be sent to an inhospitable post on the front lines of a doomed war, just like his great-uncle before him.

"It's true, I guess. Guys like you and me could get shipped off to Iraq if this thing lasts much longer," Serge says, rather generously. At twenty-two, Serge is still plausible cannon fodder. Brian is thirty-eight. He imagines there is a long line of hardier and more youthful candidates for conscription standing between him and the war. Haphazardly, Brian thinks about explaining that he could opt out anyway, just by saying, "I'm gay." The draft board would have to go knocking on other doors. But that's a detail about himself that he hasn't explicitly mentioned to Serge.

Serge and Brian have only been acquainted for two months, ever since Brian decamped from Washington to take advantage of the lower rents in Baltimore. Brian refrains from using the word unemployed to describe his circumstances. He has recently departed, under what he likes to think of as mutually agreeable circumstances (he would have quit anyway), from a junior legal position in the congressional relations department of the National Organization for Scientific Progress. The job had gone swimmingly for two years, until NOSP, with an eye toward increasing its influence among Washington's current power brokers, hired a creationist as general counsel. This led to a housecleaning in which Brian, who had once worked in Congressman Barney Frank's office, found himself standing near the exits like an exposed dust ball.

Now, with two similarly situated castaways, Brian is a founding member of a liberal think tank, the Greater Good. This entails working out of his living room on a laptop computer, printing up glossy business cards, and issuing the occasional "white paper" or press release, while he and his colleagues bandy about ideas for where they might find some money. Without much in the way of appointments, conferences, or meetings that require his attention, Brian has had time to explore downtown Baltimore, where he discovered Sergeant.

Shirtless and sweaty, Serge stood by a portable hardware store on a street corner, his eyes behind a protective shield, ready to make keys for worker bees on their way to the commuter trains that travel back and forth between Baltimore and Washington. Brian, a subtle stalker, became a regular customer, often pretending he was in a hurry to catch the train to D.C. He had spare keys made of spare keys, and spares made of keys he had found in junk drawers. He offered to get keys made for friends. He often bought new key chains. But as their acquaintance grew, he eventually allowed that he was only working "part-time," and began to idle away many an afternoon in small talk with his friend the key-maker.

Most of the day, after the morning and afternoon rush of commuters, business at Serge's hardware hut was slow. Serge spent time outside his stand, reading the sports pages and chatting with passersby, basking amiably among the pedestrians and panhandlers and gadflies who stopped to visit. The sight of him, one leg propped up on the bench, goggles hanging loose around his neck, leavened Brian's afternoons. Serge smiled knowingly whenever he greeted his people, now including Brian, who relished glimpses of sweat on Serge's chest, punctuated by the glitter of tiny flecks of brass from the key-cutter.

Soon enough, Serge noticed Brian admiring his chest and stomach on a particularly steamy August day. When Serge raised his arms to stretch, his thigh-length jeans slipped down so that his devil horns and the top of his bush showed. He did not flinch. He seemed unconcerned that the only thing preventing a full frontal nudity display—in bright daylight for all of down-town Baltimore to see—was his tight, round butt, barely holding up his jeans from the back. Brian, light-headed, gazed at Serge and mentioned something about wanting to have washboard abs like his.

"My wife likes it too," Serge said, rubbing his hand over his damp, shirtless torso. Ah, yes, his wife. Serge had mentioned her before, often in a similar context, suggesting a boundary not to be crossed. Brian imagined her as a stout woman, holding a rolling pin. *Look, but don't touch* was the message. Brian got the hint, but he had little else to do with his time, so he kept showing up, two or three days a week, to hang out drinking coffee on the plaza benches near Serge's hardware stand, ready to make small talk. He was an optimist at heart.

By the time Serge asked Brian if he liked fishing, the answer that leapt from Brian's mouth seemed as honest as it was prepos-terous.

"I *love* fishing," Brian said, with a Liza-like enthusiasm that caught Serge off guard. Brian neglected to mention that he hadn't actually been fishing since eighth grade, when his family had moved east from Michigan; the old days of fishing for perch and walleye at a cabin in the Upper Peninsula had receded into a mothballed closet of childhood memories.

Serge laughed. "We should go sometime. I like fishing in the bay, about an hour's drive from here. There's a good place for sea bass. The water's not so polluted if you go north of the city a bit."

"Yes, that would be fun. I'd like to go."

"I'm going Saturday. You wanna come?"

That's how Brian ended up in Serge's pickup, with a chorus of empty beer cans rattling in the back of the cab. Brian feels the floor panel vibrating beneath his feet, and hopes his seat is not about to fall through to the rushing pavement below.

At the shore, they walk along a thin path through rocks and bramble. The Chesapeake laps at the rocks to their left as they hike inland from the lot where Serge has parked. The flotsam washed ashore consists mostly of beer cans (some of which Serge stops to examine, before tossing aside—he's a collector), fast-food wrappers, and several used condoms. Brian hopes it isn't too obvious that his rod and reel are brand new, and finds himself scanning his equipment to make sure he hasn't forgotten to cut off price tags. Serge leads the way, in a blue tank top and his usual midlength jeans. The few hairs on the back of his calves are black and short and sexy. The farther they walk the less debris they see, and the more Brian's nausea from the truck ride subsides. They pass one lone fisherman, out on a jetty. Serge occasionally points out a landmark—the rock where he fell into the bay and nearly got swept away by the current, the place where he saw two raccoons fighting each other, a trail that leads to caves where teenagers died of asphyxiation several years ago. Each tale unveils an unmarked danger, a sign that civilization is being left behind. Eventually, Serge stops.

"Sergeant's Bay," he announces, sweeping his hand over a clearing in the shoreline, a crescent-shaped cove with a pebble beach punctuated by much larger stones.

He sets down his tackle box, takes off his tank top, and prepares his bait. He's got a jar of pork scraps, and he affixes a piece of meat to a hook, which in turn is attached to what appears to be a metallic replica of a fish head. When he casts his line out, it forms a smooth arc of filament and settles into the water almost silently. Brian's bait is a rubber frog studded with treble hooks behind a leader with a line of shiny, glimmering spoons meant to attract freshwater bass. Serge says he's never seen anyone fish using that kind of lure in the Chesapeake Bay. Brian is surprised to find his own casting is as graceful and smooth as he remembered from his childhood trips in Michigan. Even Serge seems impressed with the distance Brian gets. The lure lands with a soft plop, and Serge watches as Brian slowly reels it in and casts it out again. Brian, a fidgety person by nature, is not acclimated to the sit-and-wait style of fishing. He prefers to cast out and reel in, again and again, somewhat comforted by the thought that his floating lure isn't likely to draw any fish up from the Chesapeake's depths. While casting comes naturally to him, he'd hate to have to clean a fish.

Brian eventually takes off his shoes and socks and wades a few feet into the cool water. Serge looks at his pink feet refracted beneath the surface. Brian keeps his shirt on, sure that he'd look pudgy and pale next to Serge's lithe, brown body.

Fearing the sunlight, Brian wears a floppy hat that shields much of his face. Serge laughs at it. "You look like Mary Poppins," he says.

"Katharine Hepburn, I like to think," Brian says, but Serge's laugh is tentative. He may be unfamiliar with the reference.

They are silent for a while. Serge keeps a close eye on the tip of his rod. When Brian tires of casting, he sits on a rock next to Serge and drags figure eights in the water with his little frog, scaring away schools of panicked minnows. Occasionally he glances at the more vigilant Serge. His eyes have started to wander too. A few boats and cormorants punctuate the bay.

Suddenly, Serge takes off his shoes and steps gingerly into the water. For a moment, it seems he's preparing to strip off his jeans, but instead he leaves them on and slides into the water, dunking his head. Then he climbs back onto the rock, water dripping off his pants and the moist coils of his hair.

"Sometimes, I go swimming naked. Only late in the afternoon, when the boats are mostly gone," he says.

Don't let me stop you, Brian thinks. They smile at each other and Serge looks away.

"I told my wife about that. She says I'm crazy. I could get arrested or somebody could steal my things. But there's nobody around. Nobody cares anyway."

Just when Brian thought they were getting somewhere, *she* pops up again, wielding her rolling pin. Brian sits back against the rock, admiring the way the cool water has glazed and tightened Serge's skin, especially around his nipples. Brian's mouth waters.

"Fishing is slow in August. It's better in June, early July," Serge muses. "Maybe the fish go deeper when it's this hot. Maybe that's why the boats are all out so far."

He stands and wedges his fishing rod into a crevice in the rock that's sturdy enough to hold even if a fish does happen to take his bait.

"Let me show you something," he says, sitting up to put on his shoes. Brian follows suit. They jump from the rocks back to shore and scamper up a dry gully. Eventually, maybe a hundred yards up from the shore, they come to an area where thick slabs of concrete, ruins from some abandoned outpost of industry, break up the forest, creating their own small clearings. The two men climb up onto one of the big slabs, with sunlight piercing through the canopy of trees like stage lighting.

"This is my place. If I'm tired of fishing I come here and just sit in the sun sometimes," Serge explains. "I've never seen anyone else up here. Never even any garbage. It's weird that way. The kids don't come this far into the woods, I guess."

And it's true. The landscape seems undiscovered, frontierlike. Some of the slabs are threaded by vines. It has the feel of a lost empire in a rain forest. Serge leans back against the concrete, absorbing the sun and warmth. This time, even Brian takes off his shirt, if only to use it as a pillow behind his head. Serge pays no mind to Brian's body, at first. But Brian can't help watching as Serge hooks one thumb into the top of his jeans.

"You like me. I can tell," Serge says suddenly.

"Everyone likes you," Brian says, by way of defense.

"You like me a lot. I can tell. It doesn't matter. I don't mind."

Ah, Sherlock Holmes, how did you guess? Brian thinks.

But he can't think of anything to say. The next move is unclear to him. There's no use in denying and little benefit in admitting how he feels. He looks out toward the bay, visible as specks of rhinestone through the branches and leaves. "You are very, very beautiful and very nice too. It would be difficult not to like you," Brian says.

Serge sits up, and Brian senses that perhaps that old border guard, his wife, is about to be summoned into duty. But instead Serge says, "I'm going to do what I normally do."

He slips off his jeans so that he is completely naked and rolls up his pants to use as a cushion behind his head, as Brian has done with his shirt. Serge leans back and closes his eyes.

"I don't mind if you look at me," he says.

And Brian does look, ravenously. Serge's uncut cock is large and soft, resting in its untrimmed bed of hair. His thighs are stronger than Brian had guessed. Even Serge's face is more beautiful, framed by curls of hair splayed against the concrete. Brian leans close and smells the traces of shampoo and gasoline in his hair, then he sits up, scanning the length of Serge's body. Serge opens his eyes and smiles shyly, amused by Brian's fascination, by the power of his body to captivate.

"Okay, you can touch me a little bit if you want. I guess it's okay," Serge says.

And touch Brian does. He touches Serge's chest, with its few black hairs and exposed rib cage, his stomach, with its ridging of muscle, his hip bones, framing groin and pubic bush. Serge's cock stirs, engorges, as Brian starts caressing it, ever so lightly. Serge doesn't open his eyes. Brian props himself on one elbow, his arm grazing Serge's hips. *I've become Sergeant's wife*, thinks Brian. He is even tempted to say *I want to have your baby*, but silence seems wiser. Serge's hand rises up and he begins to run his fingers through Brian's hair. His cock is now totally hard, in front of Brian's face.

"You can do whatever you want," Serge says.

TELLING A SWITCH'S STORY

Arden Hill

Tell me you're not lazy. Make me believe it when you're lying in bed one leg against the wall, one on the dulled edge of the sheet held against the air and I am fucking you with both hands and have been for more than an hour, my shoulder already as sore as your thighs will be after I've stopped. Your breath better remind me that you're trying hard to be good, trying harder than I have to when you ease into my mouth and tell me not to lick or pull you down my throat. You tease me with the smell of your sweat and the curve of your cock just resting on my lower lip till you let me suck you off. Don't tell me now, because I like the way you bite your lip and whimper. I don't want any words from you now. But tell me later, that on the bottom you can take more fingers or bear more weight than you could if I hadn't told you to try and please me, slapped you and told you to try harder till you do.

I want to know you recognize power, because I watch you tear and build on reforming like a muscle. I watch you arch and flex, nipples rising close to my belly, trying for and reaching what you crave, what you don't want to say because you trust me to know, and I do. I'm just making you wait for it, letting you earn your satiation. It's in your veins, throbbing blue serpents beneath your still skin, when I've told you not to move. I hold you down with my eyes and nothing else because I like to see your pulse.

Tell me why you like to top me, and I will confess what the words *good boy* do when slipped into the ear that your tongue has made wet, that your mouth has made warm. Please, if it would please you. Tell me you understand the whisper of *Whatever you want*. You're right. I do have something in mind, but I already told you. It's repeated each time my unfilled mouth falls open. Flesh emphasizes where words fall short, even these words. I don't want to speak specifics, I just want you to carry me to the space that's connected to each act I've already consented to, like the flick of your crop against my dick or the first and second knuckles of your first and second fingers working into my ass.

Sometimes you give me a choice, *Faster or harder?* Other times you give me what you want and I struggle against it because resistance is a skin on pain. I like to feel it rubbing raw and you pushing into what you've had me spread with my own fingers. Maybe it's a metaphor. Maybe not. What do you want it to be? Do you like to watch me? Do you want to cover my eyes again with a black bandana? When you don't, when you let me look, I watch you. I watch looking travel between us, your eyes and mine. I don't blink. And on my knees, wrists held apart by a joiner chained so close to my face I could bite metal like a bit, I watch your reflection in the silver curve where the clamp rests to a lock.

I like to top you more than just because you want it. I want it. I think about you shoved down on your stomach when I'm biting the pillow. Looking up, seeing how much I please you, I imagine looking down at you when you're too submissive to speak, even to beg, and it pleases me. There is a space I know with you from knowing both the top and the bottom. We learn the middle, also, the flesh that is neither bone nor dripping want but there like the tenderness of a bruise under skin.

Push me over edges you know I will never be able to jump the way I desire, cross when I tell you to cross over the conflict between what you want and what you think you should. We are good, lover, at both.

THE MANOR

Andrew Warburton

I

It was paradise in the Manor. I lived there before I knew anything about life, before I tasted my first sip of beer, my first slobbery penis, my first prick of the needle, the bitterness of a drug dissolving on my tongue. The Manor had polished tile floors, and walls that smelt of disinfectant, and air full of dust blown up by the vacuum cleaners and rags the caretaker would use every morning before we got up for breakfast. We all had leather-bound cases called tuck-boxes, full up with sweets and pictures of scantily clad women, and our desks were made of the oldest, knotted oak, so rough we had to write on paper supported by our books: those simple Latin sentences about love and war, agoras and atriums, *Iulius* and *Iulia*. We wore blazers of the deepest maroon, with white stripes at the collar and the sleeves, and a coat of arms above our left breast with the motto *Aut disce aut discede*—"learn or leave."

They said the older boys lay on their backs at night and played with their penises till milk shot from the end. There must be something wrong with them, I said. That isn't normal. Don't tell me any more. I'd never experienced an orgasm, though I was seventeen years old. The closest thing to sex I'd experienced was watching Mr. Jones, the Games Master, during afternoon sport. I couldn't keep my eyes off his big, arcing thighs, and the fat ass stuffed into his tight canvas shorts, which always made the matrons blush when they walked by. One day he called me to his office. I walked through the gloomy hall to the steps where they said the "gray lady" had fallen to her death outside the library door—past the dorms to a little room I'd never seen before. He was sitting behind his desk with a smile on his face, his forearms resting on a loose pile of papers, his dark hair glistening in the light from the window through which I saw a patchwork of fields.

"Come in and shut the door," he said, his voice a lilting Welsh.

I did as he said. Before I sat down, I caught sight of myself in the mirror on the wall. I saw the light reflected off my shirt and the soft flesh at the open collar where a few dark hairs had appeared. Suddenly I was aware of how tightly my trousers were pulled around my groin and my ass, and I felt the dark eyes behind the desk crawling over me.

Mr. Jones stood and I saw his thighs bulging under the smart black trousers. His fingers were already at the zip, slowly pulling it down, pulling out his long fleshy penis. I'd never seen a man's penis before. It made my friends' and my own seem tiny. I'd never even seen my father's except through the white satin shorts he wore when he went running—and that was just a squashed, misshapen bulge; large, but nothing to shout about.

This was like a truncheon.

He reached across the desk and put his big hand on the back of my head, pulling me toward him. I could feel the warmth of his skin, the mound of his palm and the hard bones in his fingers. "I want you to put it in your mouth and blow."

I leant forward and put my mouth to the tip. It was sticky, very purple and full, as if it had been blown up with air. I brushed my tongue across it and kissed it. He shivered. It was velvety on my lips. I reached up and put one hand on his balls. The other I ran through the black, matted hairs on his stomach.

"Blow," he said huskily, and I blew. It was strange what happened then. I blew and blew and the air from my mouth seemed to fill the inside of his penis. His breath came heavy and I blew even more and his penis became more and more swollen. His balls were silky, covered in soft hairs, and they too were swollen and they just kept getting bigger and bigger. The tip of his penis pushed past my lips, filling the whole of my mouth. It was almost too big to keep inside. My tongue was too small to fit around it and it kept slipping out of my mouth. Eventually I gave up trying. I held the wet tip to my lips and continued pushing the air from my lungs, up past my throat, into his penis. Soon it resembled one of those sausage-dog balloons that the magicians used to make at my friends' birthday parties. His thighs and hips kept wriggling frantically in the air, circling as if he couldn't bear it. And his breathing was deep, and loud grunts kept escaping from his lips.

"I'm cumming," he said suddenly, and he tightened his hand on the back of my head and cried out, as if in pain. I didn't understand. Who was he talking to? There was no one else there; nowhere to go. And then it came, and finally I understood. Liquid sprayed my mouth, unlike anything I'd ever tasted before. It had the color and consistency of milk, and the taste was disgusting, like the chipolatas we threw under the table at supper time rather than eat them. But he was wiping the tip across my lips, smearing the milky substance all over them. I grimaced. It was slippery and foul-tasting, but I had to drink it down. I licked my lips clean, swallowing it all—and gradually, as if it had been punctured and the air let out, his penis returned to its normal size.

"Good boy," he said, putting it back inside his pants. "You may go."

My legs trembled as I got up. I opened the door. I took one look at his soft dark hair, glistening, with the trees and the fields behind it, but he wasn't looking at me anymore, his head was in his hands, so I went out into the corridor and shut the door behind me.

II

At the back of the Manor was a country garden surrounded by tall walls, with pear trees growing against the crumbling stone. We used to steal the pears, sink our teeth into the flesh and hide the carcasses in the bushes where no teachers would find them. There was a birdhouse too, where we'd watch the birds copulating in a patch of wasteland; there were badgers too, but they only came out at night, snorting like dogs as they mounted each other. And there was a quarry where we were forbidden to go, where purple heather grew among the rocks. And the valley we walked through to reach it was huge, the trees so tall they made patterns in the misty clouds, and the rocky stone walls were covered in moss and ivy.

I went there once with Bliss.

Bliss was the best footballer in school. He had deep brown eyes and full luscious lips and a shock of glossy, raven black hair through which he kept running his hands. He was a whiz with the ball and could keep one in the air for a whole five minutes at least, his white muscular legs flashing up and down through the drizzly rain. Every afternoon, when we came in from the wind and the muddy pitch, I followed him back to the changing rooms and watched him pull his jersey up over his head, the sweat and rain making it stick to his nipples for a moment before revealing the creamy, toned pectorals. Many a time I'd wanted to pull the tight, muddy shorts down around his thighs.

Now, hidden in the forbidden quarry, he pulled them down around his plump, white ass, and bending over, said, "I know you've been watching me. All the lads know it. Why don't you eat my ass? I want you to."

I bent down and put my face between the fleshy mounds. I pushed my tongue into his tightly puckered hole. I was blushing and quivering all over.

"Ooh," he moaned, and he wriggled his feet forward so that his ass fell back, practically sitting on my face. He put his hands either side of his ass and pulled the cheeks apart, allowing my tongue more room to maneuver—and he wriggled down again and again, his hole tasting salty and stale.

Suddenly, he seemed to press down on his bowels and I felt a great shudder run through him. Then, with a reverberating clap, a fart exploded in my mouth. The sound echoed against the valley walls, followed by Bliss's raucous laughter: "Did you really think I wanted you to eat my ass?"

I fell back against the ground and pushed myself up onto my elbows, waves of shock and shame coursing through me. I wiped at my lips. Bliss was standing above me—his majestic white thighs towering over me—holding his enormous penis in both hands. The thick veins rippled along the shaft as he worked his hands furiously up and down it. The purple head began to buck and bob in the air and his eyelids shut and he licked his lips. I could almost smell it, straining above me, and without warning, a jet of white exploded from the tip, and Bliss's handsome face contorted. He shouted hoarsely, jerking his cock all over me. I shut my eyes but it was too late. Hot, stinking cum sprayed my face.

Bliss sniggered. He shook the last drop of cum from the end of his cock onto my face and pulled up his trousers. "That's what happens to faggots who watch me in the changing room and think they can eat my ass like a goddamn girl." His cock was still large, but it was flaccid now as he squashed it back inside his shorts. He cast one last derisory glance in my direction and walked back toward the school.

I lay among the stone and the heather, wiping his hot cum from my face.

III

Classics was always my forte. My favorite teacher was Jennings. I remember the circular structure of *The Odyssey* that he would scribble, each year, in blue chalk on the wall. It was Jennings' personal theory and he was very proud of it. He would walk back and forth in front of it, tapping the board with a ruler. Then he'd plant his fat ass on the desk, displaying his muscular thighs.

The others were surprised by this display of his crotch. I could hear the sharp intake of breath as they spied the ample bulge.

I, on the other hand, was used to these displays of machismo. I matched them one for one.

Thing was with Jennings and I, we could communicate in silence—I'd spread my legs under the desk and watch him watching with perverted glee. He would drop his pen and bend to pick it up, bringing his beautiful round ass level with my eyes. Then he'd smirk.

I'd put my palms on the insides of my thighs and slowly prise them apart.

I only sucked him off once. It was in his office. His was the biggest cock I'd seen so far.

He was sitting behind his desk, playing with the end of his thick black moustache, his eyes twinkling in that damned confident way that always made my blood boil. I planted myself in the armchair opposite him.

"What can I do for you?" he said.

"It's Eliot. I've got a bit lost with the references."

He chuckled, "You're not the first." He reached up to the bookshelf where he found a copy of Eliot, *Selected Poems*, and pulled it down. As he flicked through the slim volume I looked around at his office. I'd been here a couple of times before—mostly being ticked off for writing sloppy course-works—but I'd never really *looked* at it before. It was a bit stuffy in an academic sort of way and there were all sorts of posters hanging on the walls, advertising freak shows and circuses and pulpy magazines.

He was watching me now, his dark eyes absorbing mine, his handsome, chiseled face bearing a trace of five o'clock shadow. Sometimes, like now, I couldn't even look at him without getting hard. I shifted my satchel across my lap.

"You like my stuff?" he asked.

"Yes, I love looking at people's books."

He smiled. I noticed the creases deepening either side of his mouth. He must be pushing forty, I thought, but his eyes were so bright they made him look younger.

"Look Jake, let's stop pretending, shall we? I'm too old to be playing these kind of games. I know why you're here."

I leant back in my seat. "I'm sorry?"

His smile was maddening but he said nothing. He just kept looking at me, forcing me to guess what he was about to say. Then he stood up.

The first thing I noticed was the leather belt pulled taut around his hips. Then the big shiny buckle. My eyes strayed down to his bulging fly and I saw the outline of his cock straining through the fabric.

"Come on, boy. Don't be shy. I know you're begging for it."

I spluttered, "What gives you that idea?"

"Come on Jake, I see it all the time. The way you watch me in class. To be honest it's a bit embarrassing. If you want to suck my cock, you just have to ask."

I blushed despite myself. My dick was beginning to stir. "I don't know what you're talking about, sir."

For a moment the doubt flickered in his eyes. Then he came round to the front of the desk and sat down in front of me, spreading his legs wide. His cock was hard, pressed along the length of his thigh, and his hands were warm as they slipped around my head, smoothing the hairs on the back of my neck. "I know you want it, baby." He unzipped his fly and, without warning, thrust his cock between my lips, "Get that pretty mouth round my meat."

I sucked his cock in long, delicious strokes. He purred like a giant cat, making small encouraging noises in his throat. He was very, very hard, but he fit my tongue perfectly, sliding along the walls of my mouth. His legs began to twitch and for a moment I thought he was going to cum, but then he pushed down on the back of my head, forcing my lips down the length of his shaft till they grazed the heavy balls. "That's right, baby. All the way." I spread my mouth as wide as it would go, but it wasn't enough— I was going to gag. Panicked, I tried to jerk my head back and gulp for air, but he merely held my head in place, saying, "I like it when you choke on me, baby." He thrust as hard as he possibly could, his hips pounding my lips. He was pumping my mouth as if it was some kind of sucking machine, or one of those blow-up dolls. He moaned, "I'm cumming, baby."

Steadying myself against his thighs, I waited for the onslaught of jizz. The length of his cock continued to move wetly between my lips, but the head was bucking now against the roof of my mouth. Finally it exploded—all over my tongue—flooding my mouth with its bitterness. I swallowed in great, thirsty gulps. He whistled through his teeth.

"That's a definite A-minus for technique," he said, as I fell back on the floor.

"A-*minus*? Why A-*minus*?"

"Well, next time, suck the head a bit longer. You're sure to get an A then...."

He chuckled deep in his throat and reached down to ruffle my hair.

IV

One day my maths teacher made me cry. I couldn't do my equations. I kept staring out the window at the soccer players on the pitch—their fat cocks bouncing up and down in their shorts—imagining my mouth around them.

"Something interesting out there, Jake?" shouted Mr. Bowers. "Perhaps you'd like to go outside? You're certainly not here with us."

I felt my cheeks go bright scarlet as everyone in the room turned to face me. I looked down at the squiggly lines in the textbook in front of me. I didn't have a clue what we were supposed to be doing.

In a flash Mr. Bowers was behind me, pinching my ear between his thumb and index finger, pulling back my head. I swallowed hard. "Listen boy, if you don't concentrate you'll never learn."

"Yes, Mr. Bowers."

"See me after class."

After the others had left, I stood in front of Mr. Bowers' desk, waiting for him to look up from his marking. He had neat black hair, Mr. Bowers, and a young man's body (though he must have been about forty-five). His suit fitted nicely around his chest and broad shoulders.

"Ah yes," he said finally, his blue eyes flashing up at me, "I'd forgotten about our little meeting. I'm going to teach you a lesson, Jake. A lesson I hope you won't forget."

He walked around the desk and stood beside me. I looked down at my feet, hoping this wouldn't be too intense. He was so close now his big chest was almost touching mine. I took a deep breath and put my head to the side, away from him. But his stubble grazed my cheek. He pressed his large hand against the side of my face and slipped two fingers into my mouth. "I want you to suck my fingers, Jake—and while you're doing it I want you to think about why it's important you concentrate in class. You wouldn't want me to write home to your mother, would you? Between you and me, Jake, I know she can't easily afford our fees. You wouldn't want her thinking it wasn't worth it, would you?"

I shook my head. I couldn't reply. My mouth was too full with his fingers. I sucked greedily—wanting to please him because I knew what he said was true.

"How about some extra flavor?" he said, removing his fingers from my mouth and thrusting them inside his pants. Rummaging around inside, he looked down at me, his lips twisting into a strange smile. What was he doing? Sticking a finger up his ass? When he brought his hand to my face again, it stank of sweat; there was something else too, underneath the sweat, something biting and stale. He covered my mouth with his hand and thrust the two fingers between my lips. They tasted foul this time. I almost gagged.

"That's good," he said, watching me, the length of his cock pressing into my stomach—harder all the time. Urgently, he undid his belt with one hand, and when his cock was free, he moved back and started jacking it off, his eyes flashing with excitement. "Fancy a bit of dick-sweat?" All at once he removed his fingers from my mouth and smeared the end of his cock all over them, all around the tip and under the foreskin. His fingers were moist when he brought them to my face. The fumes rose from them, reeking of cheese.

"Lick 'em."

I shut my eyes and licked them, first quickly, as if lapping them—then in great strokes. I could taste the fruity juices of his cock.

"Oh, good boy, that's good. In a minute I'll have something even tastier for you!" The smell had gone now, his fingers were squeaky clean. And his cock had grown enormously. I was sure he was about to cum.

"Wait for it, boy! It's almost here." For a moment, he seemed to squat down—then he stood up straight, his face bright red, and he pulled the fingers from my mouth. Gasping, he caught the cum that came splashing from his cock and brought the dripping hand to my mouth. I looked on, wide-eyed, as he shoveled cum onto my tongue.

"Eat it!" he said, between pursed lips.

But I couldn't. My throat was heaving, the cum sliding under my tongue. I was going to be sick.

"No you don't!" His eyes narrowed and he grasped hold of my head, rubbing the cum against my lips. I screwed up my face. I had no choice but to swallow it.

"You don't like it, do you?" he said, stepping back, watching me gag with a wide grin on his face. No longer supported, I sank to my knees, heaving up strings of pearly cum. He looked down at me and zipped up his fly. Then, as I opened my mouth to cry out, to tell him to back off, he shaped his lips into a kiss and a large, round gob of saliva fell through the air toward my open mouth, landing with a splat on my tongue. I fell back against the boards, spitting and shaking my head. I could hear his footsteps on the other side of the room, and a low chuckle from deep inside his chest.

The door opened and he was gone.

V

I was sitting with one arm out the window, overlooking the front lawn, and I couldn't stop crying because I had to leave. Someone asked me if I was okay and I said, yes, I'm fine. Eventually I carried my tuck-box out, the tiles squeaking under my cheap Clark's shoes. The corridor smelt of polish and disinfectant; that smell that made me think of Games. I thought of playing catch in the country garden where the pear trees grow against the old stone wall and the grass is kept green and low and the Games Master's thighs are big, so big, and his ass is stuffed inside his tight canvas shorts, and when he looks at me it is always softly, as if he senses I'll crumble if he stares too hard.

They sent me to a state school in the end anyway. My grades weren't good enough and my mum was poor. All things must come to an end, I thought, but why so suddenly? To be plucked from this paradise and thrown into the world before my wings were even fully grown was a fate too hard to endure! I remember the meaty taste of Mr. Jones' penis, the sweat from the crack of Bliss's spread ass; I remember the sliminess of Mr. Jennings' cum smeared across my lips and I remember Mr. Bowers' fingers.

I remember it all and I'll never forget. What better sensation is there, after all, than that of a long slippery piece of meat forced past one's lips, onto one's tongue, where it ejaculates? I still dream of it now. But it is always years later and I am much older. I stand in the shadowy doorway at the front of the Manor, licking my lips, the remembrance of salt making my mouth water. I'm dressed in a gray suit, with a long mackintosh falling all around me, with a bowler hat on my head, and I'm staring at the glistening pond, at the goldfish swimming among the lily pads in the water. I reach down my hand and trace my fingers through the surface, drawing a mouth in the water that opens wide and closes again immediately. My mouth falls open sloppily, my tongue feels the cold and I turn my back to the house so no one can see what I'm doing. I open my fly and pull out my penis. Already, it is bloated. I dash it once, twice, three times, all along the length, so that it sprays its load across the water. I convulse. I fall down on my knees and breathe out a silver cloud. I watch it expand in the wintry air. Then I look down at my fingers and see that they're covered in silver globs. I smear the globs across the grass and put my penis back inside my pants. I stand up, brushing the wet grass off my knees, and walk down the path toward the open road.

I don't look back at the Manor, though I can feel it softly breathing. Swelling—

THREE SCENES

Christopher Schmidt

ABC

"ABC," Karl explains, "means Always Be Cruising."

Karl, my new beau, is telling me about a nutty, "slutty" friend who operates on the ABC principle, adapted from a real estate mantra, Always Be Closing. We're in bed when Karl mentions this, and although he's not advocating ABCing *per se*, the phrase has a suggestive afterlife. I worry it over as I would a line of poetry—unconsciously, walking down the street—or as a tongue might return, compulsively, to the irresistible jagged tooth.

As I ponder the phrase, unlikely associations occur: "Always Be Cruising" and Alice B. Toklas. Orthographical cousins, they occupy opposite ends of the queer spectrum, steadfast Alice frowning on her promiscuous relation.

ABC is elementary; it marks the beginning of learning. ABD (a word I hear a lot of lately) does not quite end a lengthy education. Like "All But Dissertation" status, the interminability of that "always" depresses a little. In Dante's *Inferno*, the sodomites, "puckering their brows on us like an old tailor on the eye of a needle," race around the seventh circle of hell to avoid being singed by the flames chasing them. They are *forever* cruising. Dante's lesson: every choice is its own punishment.

Karl is in South Carolina, visiting his family. Left to my own devices, I am at the gym, ABCing. Cruising at the gym may signal a failure of the imagination—who hasn't fantasized about sex in the locker room?—but why reinvent the wheel? I once picked up a trick on the subway and it didn't end well.

By the dumbbells, a tall man with glasses and dark, curly hair works out with his trainer. He's Brobdingnagian, almost as tall as Karl (six foot six), maybe broader. At first my interest in him is aesthetic: he styles his hair big—to make his small head look proportionate to his body? And was it always so, or did muscle building ruin his proportions? I'm amused such a big man should require a trainer, a staff to support him, as if he were a balloon in the Macy's Thanksgiving Day parade. At this point, I've been looking his way for some time, and the man looks back, not incurious. I look again, *hard*, screwing my eyes into his, and relish the perversity of cruising him *because* he reminds me of Karl. ABC = Absent Boyfriend Counterfeit.

In the drawer of my bedside table lies a little tome called *The ABC Book*, by Maurice Vellekoop. In this "homoerotic primer," each letter of the alphabet is illustrated by a sexy watercolor tableau ("A is for astronauts" who sixty-nine in zero gravity). On the book's cover, a seated adolescent student snakes his foot up the pant leg of the teacher standing over him. The teacher, I think, is cute. Then I realize he wears the same outfit (checked white shirt with rolled up sleeves, brown tie) that I recently wore on my first day as a college English instructor. Modeling my pedagogy on porn! In a nightmare scenario, I see myself walking into class, the book trailing me like an errant piece of toilet paper. I banish *The ABC Book*, throw it deep under my bed.

The mechanics of cruising can be laborious. In the locker room, I arrange myself behind my new Brobdingnagian prospect, then pretend to ignore him. I notice, or think I notice, his attention flickering back to me. Then a ballet of loitering, as our cruise proceeds in fits and starts. In a tacky move, I haunt the sauna; indifferent, he passes on to the showers. Later, toweling off, I again notice him at the mirror, fishing something out of his eye: me!

But in our leapfrog of pause-and-wait, fantasy dissipates like weak perfume. He stalls near the exit of the gym. Irresolute, cowardly, I roll past without stopping. I look back too late and spot my trick walking the opposite direction—heading home, I imagine, to an expectant, loyal boyfriend.

Fuck Journal

Day 0 • Airport-arrived, I collapse, all thin skin and angles. I am flying to meet the BF's family. In the bathroom behind BK (home of the Whopper), some fag has his poodle out—its ass poised above a tile diaper—coaxing canine excrement. "No shit," says Leif when I relay the scene.

Onboard, I ponder *fucks*. Arid airplane air provides the perfect environment for viruses to take root. Note to self: procure Zicam to lube nose holes. Membranes need moisture.

Day 1 • Morning headache augurs *fuck*. Move fast and pain rails to cranium's leeward side, intense and loud, like kids tumbling in the backseat. We are driving on Highway 1, near Bodega

Bay (no kids). Hypochondro, I am always divining *fucks*, rarely succumbing to them. I nip buds, *fucks*. Heavy-lidded, I tell Leif, "Tippi Hedren is the mother diva because she gave birth to Melanie," (then recommend the DVD: better than the birds are Tippi's screen tests.) By the church Hitch filmed, a sedan pulls up. Out step two middle-aged men, unfashionably shod. The tall one, brandishing an arm sling over red flannel, scans me through the windshield, grins.

Races across Duncan's Landing cove leave me fevered, phlegmy. From the peak above, our despoiling is writ in eight footprint lines crossing the virgin sand. Wind up, *fuck*, I layer on the wool.

By night, my *fuck* announces his occupation with a hoarse throat, aided by the wet *fuck* of this northern clime. Our lighthouse bedroom, "off the grid," lacks heat.

Day 2 • A *fuck*'s calling card: flushing sneezes, Sahara eyes, a gummy ledge above the gullet, mucus that sticks and would stink, if I could smell.

Day 3 • Even one *fuck* in ten years is very bad, counsel macrobiotic gurus. Inflammatory information. Contagion fears. Leif's mom Sylvia pushes barley grass and Chinese herbs, tells me to pocket vitamin C. Was she a good mother? What's her angle? Is she my angel? "Your mother's a little *fucker* than I expected," I tell Leif. "But I like her."

Outside, nine cats spend lives huddled atop a hot tub cover. Nature run amok: when Sylvia leaves the house, she turns on talk radio to scarecrow raccoons from the pantry.

Day 4 • After tennis, ill timed, I study monologuists on a white shag carpet, shades of *The Sandpiper*. "What have you been up

to?" Leif asks me. Mike Albo, my alibi. In shivers, I ponder a
tongue's fossil poetry: we call it *fuck* because it makes you *fuck*,
not because growing *fuck* gives you one, that wives' tale. Quoth
Charles Ludlam: *throw another faggot on the fire*. At dinner, I
fuss with my *fuck* fish, feel nauseous.

Day 5 • I'm better. With each tissue blown, I declare this one the
last. This one the last. This one the last. Fuck this *fuck* already!

The sun lemon warm, but I'm still *fuck*. I try on words
for it: damp *fuck*, *fuck* around the edges, fresh *fuck*. A trip to
Armstrong Woods steals us from the sun: bone-chilling fuck.
"Is this where *The Return of the Jedi* was filmed?" I demand of
this attenuated wood trap. Then nail my folly: "I bet it is." We
spy Icicle Redwood, aptly named. Eucalyptus trees drop fruit I
smash underfoot.

Later, I ask Leif how I merit with Mom. "Your lack of tree-
love was a mark against you." He mimes a checklist, licks his
air-pencil. "You gotta love nature here."

I slip Leif, also with *fuck*, contraband Tylenol. (Don't tell
Sylvia!)

At Guerneville, men with rictus make eyes at my guy.

Day 6 • The parents? The undressed portrait windows? The
crevice in our futon, suggesting cleavage? Our *fucks*? Or the
moon-bare California *fuck*, keeping us from fucking?

Top/Butt
Born of sunlust, bus runs to sub-Boston porn moor, horny
homo zoo. Looks stun. No frumps, no fops, just buff studs
burnt brown. Luc, uncut, hunts cut cock. Jock, hung, lucks on
smooth boy cunt, round rump up on dun outcrop. Coy youth
sucks thumb, sub for schtup. Jock's pud pulls north. Jock stubs

youngun's mouth, swoons. Put out, Luc ducks bud's fuck. (Luc's wont: most lust.) Soon Luc spots humongous chub on pup slut Todd. Luc's succubus guns. Our two gods mushroom. Todd pulls Luc's hood. Luc flops Todd, rubs Todd's rump, drums Todd's knot, churns Todd's rut, tugs Todd's butt. Thus room, sucks nuts. Todd grunts, tough to bottom. Luc lobs sputum up Todd's duct: unctuous. Todd succumbs. Luc mounts, pounds Todd's dog. Bum rush! (No condom?) Todd pouts, Todd coughs. To Luc: Too rough! To Todd: Shut up! Crowds form. Luc pumps, pulls out, punch-fucks: Wow! Luc undocks, spurts globs of ghoul grub (cum) on buns. Luc's spunk, cock drop south. Dusk. Luc glows, Todd numb.

UNMASKED

Syd McGinley

"Alan, you're full of it!"

"I hate Halloween. I hate the masks. I don't like not knowing who people are."

I pinch him hard. We've only been seeing each for a few months, but I already know that's bullshit. "You faked last week when I had my Zorro mask on?"

He leers at the memory, but says, "That was different. I knew it was you and it was hot imagining who might be there, but I don't like really not knowing."

I'm astride him, but I sit back on my heels. "You're scared?"

He nods. It's funny to see him freaked. He's six feet four inches of tanned muscle, with a Marine haircut. *Jarhead*, I whisper when I fuck him, and he can't resist or retaliate.

"And clowns, but worse, those George Bush masks." He shivers.

He's so disconcerted. Hand on heart, I promise not to subject him to any masks.

"And I hate costumes."

"Are you sure you're gay? How can you not want to dress up? Or go to the haunted house? There's an AIDS benefit there after the parade. I heard there's Phelps in Hell! And the Santorum and Satan Show! Frist-Fuckers of America!"

"Hunter, get it through your fucking head: I *hate* Halloween."

"Has Wicca Jane hexed you?"

Wicca Jane and her girlfriend live downstairs. The entryway they share with Alan is strewn with amulets and herb bundles. He usually pokes fun at them.

"I know it's not real, but it's freaky."

"At least come to Ray's masked ball? He's dying to meet you. You haven't met any of my friends yet."

He's adamant. He'll keep the front lights off and hole up in his kitchen until the trick-or-treaters are gone. He knows he's being silly, and he teases me by saying he knows he'll be safe because Jane will charm their entry before she goes to her Samhain ceremonies. He's cute when he flirts. So, although I know he's distracting me on purpose, I give up. Just on the argument, not on us. Besides, I'm hard again. Arguing—even bickering—gets us hot. I'm still astride his waist. I clamp my heels on his hips and bend forward until I'm doing a push-up over his face.

If he won't say what I want to hear, then he doesn't need to be talking. It always surprises him that I'm smaller than he is, but I often get to top him. He's not pleased, but hasn't objected yet. I suspect revenge will come, but until then I'll use his good nature as much as I can.

My dick's already grazing his throat, and he's swallowing while trying to protest.

I laugh. "I know you don't deep-throat, Alan, but if you

won't come out to play, then I'll need to get my fun here."

He says something choked that I interpret as "not fair," but I'm pushing harder and deeper. Alan's hands are cupping my balls and probing my hole in an attempt to make me shoot sooner. Poor Alan, I came earlier, and I'm deliberately being a slow shot. He doesn't like this, but he's fucking awesome at eating meat. He could swallow a foot-long frank and not blink. He takes pride in his cocksucking even when the tears are in his eyes from a ramming. I repeatedly hit his gag reflex and pause to feel his soft palate quiver on my cockhead.

Fuck! He's got his finger in my ass, and has hit the sweet spot. I spurt in his throat, and stay deep for the last spasm to pay him for triggering me sooner than I wanted.

He may hate deep-throating, but he's a slut for sperm, and nurses at my shrinking dick to get it all.

"Fuck, Alan, don't, man. You know that feels too—ah fuck."

He's flipped me, and is tormenting my cock and balls. They're too sensitive, and I'm squirming and pleading in no time.

"Back off about Halloween, Hunter—I'm warning you."

I nod. At that moment I'd agree to anything, but later I realize he took a Halloween deal instead of fucking me while I was helpless. He hasn't had my ass yet. I don't give that up easily. I'll bottom for the right sort of guy, which is just as well as I invariably fall for other tops. I'm not sure yet if Alan's one under that sweet-natured exterior. He may really be just a big old jarhead looking for a daddy.

Now Halloween is here, and I'm making one last try. I'm not breaking my promise, but it's fair enough to try one more time to get him to just Ray's party. After all, I've skipped the parades and the benefits, but surely a party with friends is different? Alan's good-natured about it, but still says: no. He distracts me

with the new canapés he learned to make in class this week—
he's gone back to school as a culinary student—then coaxes me
into bed. I know he's trying to please because he rolls right over
without our usual wrangling about who's the real top. I don't
care why he's presenting his hole—I fuck him hard. Afterward,
I still want to go out.

"Go, don't stay in because I'm hung up."

I give up, but still squeeze him before I get out of bed. "Okay
babe, I'll come by tomorrow. I'll leave directions to Ray's on the
coffee table—in case you change your mind."

Just minutes into the masked ball and I miss Alan. *Ball* is a gran-
diose term: it's a seething mass of smeared makeup and parade-
battered costumes crammed into Ray's loft. Everyone's talking
about the haunted house. It sounds even better than I imagined.
Ray's a six-foot-tall skinny black drag queen, so he's both scary
and convincing as Condi Rice in her *Matrix* storm trooper outfit.
It's fun, but I've seen enough. I turn to Alan to say, "Let's go"
but of course he's not with me. Shit, I must be falling for him if
I'd rather be home with him than out on my favorite night.

I slide out of the party, and head to his place. I know he'll
ignore the doorbell even though all the ankle-biters are home
with sugar highs by now. The porch light's off to keep trick-
or-treaters away and I search for the door handle. Something
scratches my face. I yelp and freeze. It hits my scalp. I inch my
hand to my cell—it has a penlight—and point it. Fuck. An herb
bundle to protect the entry. I'll kill Wicca Jane. I let go of speed
dial, and use the penlight to go up Alan's stairs. He'd shyly given
me a key a few days ago. He's awful sweet for such a big lug.

I'm not surprised his lounge is dark—he'll still be in the
kitchen absorbed with new recipes. I've taken off my mask; I
keep promises although he's spoiled my Halloween. Most years

I spend all October creating something grotesque and fantastic. This year I couldn't summon the interest. I knew all along Alan wouldn't come, and without him it seemed pointless. Dispirited, I'd defaulted to a generic Zorroesque costume—plastic sword, tight pants, boots, and open shirt. It was okay, but my heart wasn't in it. Shit! Now my heart's in my mouth! A dark shape looms backlit in the doorway. I scream: there's a monster in Alan's kitchen!

The kitchen light snaps off and a hand on my nape draws me in. My knees are Jell-O. The creature is huge—I'm five-eight and it's a foot taller. It pushes me down to my knees. The kitchen is stark black-and-white in moonlight. All I see is silhouette: a square head and lumpy neck. From my knees my perspective is distorted, and then my view's blocked by crotch.

Whoa! Monsters are in proportion all over! I admit it, I'm a slut; I perk up when I realize why I'm on my knees. My eyes adapt. The hands on my shoulders are green-tinged, but the cock before me is honey colored. And tastes familiar—I grab Alan's ass and slurp at his hard-on. Before I lose myself, I remind myself to lie later and say I knew it was Alan before I started the blow job. I apple-bob for his balls, but he tugs my hair and returns my mouth to his rigid Franken-pole. His bent knees let his prick slide into my throat and he thrusts. I gag, but keep my hands on his butt. I knead his glutes and tickle his hole. He roars and shoots.

I sputter, then murmur, "Ah! Sweet mystery of life..."

He cracks up. "Are you ever serious, Hunter?"

"How can I be? I'm in breeches blowing Franken-cock."

He flips on the lights. Platform shoes give him those crucial four extra inches.

"Why are you dressed up?" A doubt assails me. What if he had a date and *I hate Halloween* was a ruse?

"Thought I'd try Ray's—for you—you looked so puppy dog earlier."

I'm abashed, aware I suspected him unjustly, and that I dove for his prick before I knew who he was. He must have been thinking ahead if he had even a basic Frankenstein costume ready. I've been sulking all month while he's been battling his demons.

Still. "Puppy dog!" I say indignantly. I squeal as he swats my ass.

"Breeches suit you, but better off." He hauls my breeches down. My knee-high riding boots stop them. He catches my prick in his green palm and caresses me until it strains toward him. He pulls my shirt over my head, but my hands stick at the buttoned wrists. He makes no move to undo them. I'm bound knee and wrist by my own costume, with my face hidden in shirt.

I'm helpless as Alan drags me to the sofa and onto his lap. He spanks my ass, flips me over, strokes my prick, turns me back again and slaps harder and harder until I writhe. He torments my asscheeks until they tingle and pulls on my cock until I beg him to finish me. He's mean and succumbs to the inevitable trick-or-treat jokes as he slaps and strokes.

"Which is which Hunter? Do you even know?"

I've slid half off his knees and he can access my prick with just a reach around.

He tickles my cockhead: "Trick." Slaps my ass: "Treat."

He pulls the shirt from my face. He stares into my eyes and works my shaft.

"Just a trick, Hunter?"

"No," I groan.

"Then what?"

I wriggle. Why the hell do all my relationships end up with men discovering I'm a bottom at heart?

Alan slaps me hard again. "What, boy?"

"Treat?" I venture, hoping he just wants the other half of the joke. Fuck! He's slapped my balls. He stops spanking me or stroking me and watches me fight with my pain and dignity. Alan wipes my tears with my shirt.

"Come on boy, I've unmasked you. You're not the tough guy you say you are. I heard you squeal when Jane's sage bundle hit you, and you screamed like a girl when you saw me. You were on your knees for a big cock in a second, and you're crying from a little spanking and a tiny ball slap."

I'm not the world's smartest guy. I say, "At least I'm not afraid of a children's holiday."

Alan's affectionate good humor evaporates in a second. He throws me off his lap and I'm on the floor on my hands and knees. He grabs my Zorro sword and slashes it against my ass.

I howl. It may only be a toy, but, shit, it stings.

"I know who I am boy, and I'm man enough to admit my fears. Are you?"

He hits me again, and I crawl away as fast as my clothing-bonds allow. He strides after me, switching at me. Damn, if only Wicca Jane were home. Surely he wouldn't do this to me then? The calm part of my brain says: *Of course he would.* If he's already doing this, nothing would stop him from gagging me. I finally get enough of a grip to stop crawling. I know I have to stay still and let him finish venting his anger on my ass. My attempts to escape are only fueling his anger and provoking his desire.

I hear him laugh when I lean my forehead against the cool glass of the coffee table and stay obediently still as he takes a few more swipes at my tender ass.

"Do you know who you are now, Hunter?"

"Yes," I whisper. I turn around and rest my face on his monster shoes. "Your boy."

"I could get to like Halloween," he says. "So long as you remember from now on who's who, and drop your act. Hunter: you've been caught."

BURLINGTON

Phillip Mackenzie, Jr.

The phone rang. Brendan jumped and stabbed himself farther onto my tongue, then moaned and twitched while I lazily jacked his cock.

"Do you need to get that?" he muttered after the third ring.

I pulled my face out of his ass for a second to say, "Machine'll get it."

Before he could respond, I heard my own voice say, "It's Josh, leave it at the beep," followed by Rob's voice saying, "Dude, pick up the phone." I kept eating Brendan out as Rob chanted, "Pick up, pick up, pick up, pick up," for a few minutes and then said, "Dude, I know you're there, you never go anywhere."

I snorted. Brendan jumped again, looked wildly at me. He thought Rob was his boyfriend, and hearing his voice on the phone like that freaked him out, so I gave his cock an extra-strong stroke that made him groan and shudder. His pucker clamped down on my tongue and I shook my head back and forth like a dog going after a gopher and he started making this puffing sound he does when he's ready to come.

"Dude," Rob was saying, "I have to go to South Carolina tomorrow. My uncle or second cousin or something, you know, one of those old guys, died, so I have to go to the funeral and you're coming with me."

Brendan was pumping his hips and his dick was getting harder in my hand, and his hole was really opening up to my tongue. I started to get drippy myself, so I started jacking myself with my free hand.

"Anyway, call me," Rob said. "I figure we'll leave in the morning... Dude, I know you're there listening, pick up the phone. Fuck you then, who has an answering machine anymore anyway. Later."

He hung up and I spit on my hand and really laid into Brendan and in a few seconds he blew all over my knuckles and my bed, which meant I had to do laundry again.

"I like road trips," Brendan said when he caught his breath.

"I hope you get to take one sometime," I said shoving my goopy hand into his mouth.

After I got Brendan out the door I picked up the phone.

"KwikKopyKorner, Brian speaking, how may I help you?"

"Yeah, hey Brian, it's Josh," I said, looking down at my bed and deciding never to buy a dark blue bed spread again. "I can't make it in tomorrow."

"Really?" He started getting that ferrety sound to his voice that always made me want to deck him. "Because you know you're actually supposed to be here right now, so it's really great that you remembered to call about tomorrow."

"That doesn't really make any sense, Brian, do you know that?" I said.

"You know what doesn't make sense, Josh?" I could see

him in my mind, his face all red, with a little prissy half smile, looking like he was about to start pounding the receiver on the desk. "What doesn't make sense is you. If you want this job, to keep this job, it might make more sense if you changed your attitude."

"Right," I said. "I guess that means I don't really want this job."

"You know what—" Brian's voice went all Doppler effect as I hung up the phone.

I called Rob back.

"Were you fucking somebody?" he asked me.

"No," I answered fairly truthfully. "So is this going to be all dark suits and funeral homes or can we log some country club time?"

"Definitely. Golf. Pool. Beer."

"So who was it who died?"

"Like I know?" he said. "We're related to half the people in the fucking state."

"That's why you're retarded," I said.

"Funerals and weddings down there are just excuses for family reunions. The only people who get noticed and remembered are the ones who don't show up, and I like to keep Mom happy. If you think that's, what was your word, retarded, well that just shows the depth of evil in your dead black heart. I pity you."

He was serious about keeping his mom happy, which is kind of funny because he's really an asshole in a gangly white trash rock star sort of way. Actually he isn't any of those things besides gangly, but the way he talks you'd think he didn't give a shit about anything. Mostly we just hang out and watch Comedy Central and get burnt. I'm the only person I know who likes him. I know if I ever needed anything, he'd give me the shirt off someone's back. Plus his family is fucking loaded, so it's top-shelf booze all the way if you know what I mean, and all we had to do was put on a suit for a couple of hours. Sweet deal.

He picked me up about ten the next morning, pulling up outside my building in a fucking Nova. An old one.

"You have a trust fund as big as a Hilton cunt," I said, tossing my bag into the back. "What the fuck is this?"

The front seat was a grimy off-white, punched with holes out of which fell Styrofoam stuffing. It smelled like mold and rust.

He laughed, and pulled away from the curb.

Rob shops at Salvation Army and buys his cars from these scary dealerships on Pulaski Highway up in Baltimore. Then he tricks them out with Bose speakers and drives down the road with the windows shaking and enough black smoke coming out the ass end to burn a new hole in the ozone layer. He thinks it's cool, and all he does when I tell him he's a dick is laugh.

"You were fucking Brendan yesterday," he said, as we got on I-95 headed south.

"I didn't fuck him exactly," I said, glancing over to see if he was pissed. "Did he tell you?"

"No, he called me last night and was acting weird, so I kind of figured."

"He said he hadn't seen you in two weeks, you hadn't called him back. I felt bad for him."

"I don't care." Rob looked at me and grinned. "I really don't. Actually I kind of like it. It's cool."

Not really. Not really. But I didn't say anything, because what's to say?

We'd been on the road for about five hours, and it was in the heat of the afternoon when the shit-heap Nova lurched and went *bang*, and then started going *bang bang bang bang bang* really loud and fast. All this white-hot-smelling smoke came pouring out the back and we coasted onto the side of the road, where it died.

"That's fucked up" Rob said looking at me sideways.

"Yeah, big shock too, because I thought this car was in really good shape," I said.

"Oh, sorry. I guess we should have taken your car. Except, wait…you don't have one."

We were sitting on the shoulder of I-85 with eighteen-wheelers and distracted parents driving minivans flying by us. It was about ninety degrees, and the shit-heap didn't have air-conditioning even when it was running. None of this seemed to be bothering Rob, who was grinning at me like, "Isn't this fun?" but I was ready for a change of scenery pretty fast.

I could see an exit about a quarter mile up the road, and there was a big truck stop sign towering over it, so we headed in that direction, hoofing along through weeds and tossed away Burger King bags, with hot exhaust and road dust whipping us in the eyes every time a truck blasted by.

Okay, this is where I do the long-story-short part. They couldn't do anything to help us at the truck stop because a crappy broken-down Nova is not a truck, but we did find out that we were in Burlington, North Carolina. For whatever that was worth. I told Rob we should find a car dealer and buy a new one, just leave the Nova to finish rotting, but he looked at me like I had just kicked his puppy.

The mechanic at the truck stop called this guy he knew who had a repair shop and he said he'd tow the car in and see what he could do. We walked back to the car, and after about a half an hour this guy showed up in a tow truck and hauled us down this *Deliverance*-looking dirt road to where he had a garage attached to his house.

So, at about four P.M., there we were, sitting cross-legged on a concrete slab, waiting and smoking and sweating. When the mechanic's kid, a scrawny buck-toothed redheaded thing took to driving the riding lawnmower in reverse up and down the driveway, Rob looked at me with wide eyes and said, "That is seriously fucked up," and got up and walked into the shop.

I just lit another smoke and watched the little *Hills Have Eyes* creepshow ride back and forth some more, until Rob came out and said, "Let's go."

"Where?"

"Don't know, but this place creeps me out and the car won't be done until tomorrow."

"Well, okay, but…" I got up and walked after him down the driveway. "Wait up Rob, I mean, do you even know where you're going?"

"Not really, but we came through town on the way here, so we'll go there unless you want to stay here and play with ratboy." He jerked his head toward the kid.

"Well, can we grab some of our shit first?"

As we walked down the road with the sun in our eyes and backpacks on our backs, I decided that Burlington, North Carolina is a useless assfuck of a town that has no reason for existing. The only thing we found after fifteen minutes of walking was a Wal-Mart.

I hate Wal-Mart. Not only because it's like a virus that sucks the life out of every town it infects, but because it's also like a church rummage sale grown to grotesquely horrible proportions. Heaps of tires, flyswatters, liquid plumber, ugly appliquéd sweatshirts, monstrous bags of Styrofoam plates and DVDs of *Left Behind* assault you as you stumble through in a drooling daze of hypnotized mass consumption.

Rob grabbed a cart and started throwing stuff in it, just a random mix of crap we walked past, until we found the bathroom, then he left the cart outside the door, and we went inside to wash up.

We'd been in there like fifteen seconds when the door popped open, and this Wal-Mart automaton bustled through the door, all official in his white shirt and blue vest/smock with its lame-ass fucking smiley face leering at us. He pulled up short and stared at Rob and me, and in the seconds between his appearance and when he spoke, I could tell that the presence of two shirtless guys with muscles in his bathroom was something he was going to jerk off to later that night. But only after the lights were out.

"Can I help you gentlemen?" he asked uncertainly.

Rob turned around and looked at him without speaking while he continued to wash under his arm with his balled up T-shirt.

"I don't know, Justin," he said, looking at Justin's name tag, "what did you have in mind?"

"Are you...homeless?" Justin asked, worry all over his cute face.

And he was cute. Blond and blue-eyed and with an accent that made him sound dumber than a box of hair. And if anyone can make a stupid Wal-Mart smock look interesting enough to make you think they might be worth seeing out of it, well Justin did.

"Are we homeless, Josh?" Rob asked me. "Justin wants to know if we're homeless."

"We're not homeless, we just smell like it," I said.

Rob ran one hand over that sexy patch of hair between his pecs, over his nipple and into his left armpit, before holding out his hand to Justin.

"Do you want to smell?"

"No!" Justin practically shouted, lurching backward a step.

But he did want to, and he knew that we knew that he did. Rob and I both laughed.

"Oh, Justin, you look like dinner. But right now we need a hotel. Do you know where Josh and I can find a hotel?"

"Um, well, there are a bunch of them. Which one did you want?"

"The one with the shower and the beds."

"That's stupid," Justin said. "They all have that."

"Really? Well which one do you think we should stay at, Justin?" Rob said, smiling his sexiest rock star smile. At this point, the only person who didn't know that Rob was going to fuck Justin was Justin.

"I can give you directions," he offered.

"Well, see, Justin, that's a problem," I said. "Rob's car is in the shop, so we have no way to get there."

"Unless you wanted to give us a ride," Rob said like it had just occurred to him.

And of course there was no way little Justin wasn't going to do that, so we waited outside Wal-Mart until Justin got off work about an hour later. We watched him walking toward us talking to some fat chick.

"Justin. Where's that hotel you're taking us to?" Rob barked across the parking lot.

The fat chick jumped and stared before hurrying away and Justin turned red and I laughed before realizing it wasn't really that funny.

Anyway, we all loaded into Justin's Tercel, me in the back, and Rob riding shotgun, where he kept one hand on the back of Justin's head the whole way to the Best Western.

"Come on in, Justin," Rob said when we got there. "You can drive us to dinner after we check in."

He smirked at me, as Justin said, "Oh, okay," with a lost look on his bunny face.

Once we'd checked in and gotten the key, Rob threw his backpack across the room as we walked in; it landed on the bed nearest the bathroom. Almost in the same motion he pulled his shirt over his head and then kicked his shoes off. With his back to us he dropped his pants and bared his pale muscly ass. Justin's eyes bulged, and I threw myself on the other bed and turned on the TV as Rob walked into the bathroom and shut the door.

"He's nice, huh?" Justin said.

"No, actually he's not. Not at all."

Rob turned on the shower and immediately started singing "Old Soul Song for the New World Order," wailing out "They go wiiiiild, they go wiiild..."

Justin kept talking, telling me about the girl in the Wal-Mart parking lot whose name was Stephanie and something else stupid and boring. He was in the middle of telling me a story I wasn't listening to about his sister who had just had a kid named Kyle, when Rob walked naked into the room and snapped, "Shut up, Forrest, and get over here and suck my cock."

Well, little Justin jumped off that bed like someone had shot him and stared at Rob, who had his fist wrapped around his dick, which was growing fast and starting to look a really pissed-off red.

"What?" Justin blurted.

"Suck it. Just fucking suck it you stupid little hick, you know you want to."

"I do not," Justin squawked. "I never said that."

Rob walked over to him, got up close, put a hand on the back of Justin's head, and kissed him, hard. The kind of kissing Justin dreamed about. Rob pulled away, and smiled at him. Justin smiled back.

"Now. Suck. My. Cock."

Even though he tried to act all Sunday School you could tell he'd done it before because he dropped to his knees and swallowed Rob's prick down to the hairy root without so much as blinking.

Rob clamped one hand on the back of Justin's blond head and rode his face hard, steering him and pushing him while Justin scrambled around like a crab running backward until Rob had him backed up against the bed. With one foot on the floor and one on the bed, Rob pounded Justin's throat, filling the room with slurping and moaning and the sound of Rob saying, "Yeah, take it you little bitch."

I kicked back in the chair and put my feet up on the useless Formica table that was sitting there for no good reason, and watched.

Rob grabbed Justin by the arms and yanked him to his feet. He pulled the kid's shirt off and went to work on his pants. His stiff prick bounced around crazily as soon as it broke free of his underwear. Rob grabbed it, and jacked it a few times. Justin let out a surprised grunt and then a little whimpering yell and fired off all over Rob's thighs.

I laughed.

Rob kept jacking him until his knees went out and he fell backward onto the bed.

"I'm sorry, I didn't mean to go so fast," Justin said.

"Clean it up," Rob said, standing there, legs apart, Justin-spooge trickling down his thighs.

Justin looked around for a towel or something, but Rob grabbed the back of his head, and said, "With your tongue, fuck nuts."

Rob looked over at me, his dick poking out, red and angry, and winked.

"Go kiss Josh," he said to Justin.

Justin looked at me from down below Rob's balls.

Rob pushed him toward me, and he crawled across the carpet, and knelt next to me. I leaned down and kissed him, tasted the cum on his lips, forced my tongue into his mouth, and ran one hand over his smooth chest.

"Take his clothes off," Rob said. He was sitting on the bed watching us.

Justin's hands were shaking, as he untied my shoes, slipped my T-shirt over my head, pulled my jeans off. My dick lay against my stomach, half-hard, almost interested.

Justin looked at it, reached for it, but I pushed his hand away.

Rob looked at me and smiled.

"Bring him here," he said, and I stood, and lifted Justin in my arms, carried him to the bed. I sat, Justin in my lap, and played with his sticky pecker while Rob rooted around for a condom. Justin started getting hard, and I kissed him. Rob tossed me a bottle of lube, and I opened Justin up and got him wet and ready. I was starting to get hard.

I pulled him into my arms, his back to my chest, and I pulled his legs up and back around my ears. He looked up at me, and I winked at him, just as Rob drove himself all the way into the kid with one stroke.

Justin went stiff as a board and then cut loose with a scream they must have heard all the way back at the Wal-Mart. Rob laughed and pulled out and slammed back in and then started fucking Justin like he was trying to saw him in half.

I watched Justin's face and almost felt sorry for him and mad and jealous at the same time. I held him and played with his nipples, and kissed him and rubbed my cock into his back, and jacked him the rest of the way hard while Rob huffed and snorted and pounded away above him. After a few minutes Justin started moaning and then got louder and louder until he was screaming "Oh my god fuck me," and clawing at Rob's shoulders.

"You like that huh?" Rob said, leaning into him, looking at me, fire in his eyes. I felt Justin shudder as Rob drove even farther into his guts, and I could feel it, how it hurt like hell at first, and then paid off with the kind of eye-rolling, can't breathe or talk or move prostate-battering that feels so fucking good you know you're getting closer to God. It was always better this way, with Rob. Not that he knew it. Or would have cared.

Justin thrashed around, wild-eyed and sweaty in my arms, while Rob pounded his compact butt into complete surrender, and then finally pulled out and straddled Justin's chest.

"Open your mouth, baby," he said, and Justin did as he was told.

Rob grunted once and then a jet of cum shot out of the flared red-purple head of his cock and hit Justin on the cheek. Then another shot over him and landed on me, and then Rob slammed himself into Justin's mouth and dumped the rest of his load down his throat, while I stroked harder on Justin's boner, which was twitching and dripping and ready to fire. He moaned wetly from around Rob's spurting dick, and bucked his hips up, made strange wild noises as his second load iced my fingers and dripped onto his belly.

Rob rolled off Justin's face and collapsed on the bed next to him. I slid up onto the other side of him, wrapped my arms around him, and kissed him a little while he came down. I didn't cum. I never did. It would have been more than I needed.

Rob rolled over onto his side facing Justin and reached down and gave his wet pecker a little tug.

"Did you like that, kid?" he asked, perfunctorily nice now that his nuts had been emptied.

Justin nodded and tried to kiss Rob, but Rob pulled away, and looked across the boy's body at me.

"That's sweet, Justin," he said, "but Josh is hungry. Where are you taking us to dinner?"

ABOUT THE AUTHORS

DALLAS ANGGUISH is an Australian writer whose stories and prose have appeared in the anthologies *Dumped*, *Bend, Don't Shatter* and *Between the Palms 2* as well as in the online journals Retort Magazine and Lodestar Quarterly. His full-length book of travel stories and memoir, *Anywhere but Here*, was published by Showpony Press in February 2006. He lives with his partner and two naughty cats in a small rural town in the eastern state of New South Wales.

JONATHAN ASCHE says: "I know it's more marketable to label my stories as 'erotica,' but I'm more comfortable thinking of them as pornography, albeit good pornography." His short stories, be they erotica or porn, have appeared in *Playguy*, *Inches*, *Torso*, *Honcho*, *Men* and *In Touch for Men*, and have been featured in the anthologies *Friction 3*, *Three the Hard Way*, *Manhandled*, *Buttmen 2* and *3*, *Best Gay Erotica 2004* and *2005* and *Hot Gay Erotica*. He is also the author of the erotic novels *Mindjacker* and *Moneyshots*. Asche lives in Atlanta with his husband, Tomé, and their neurotic pets.

MICHAEL CAIN is thirty-five. He lives where he grew up, in northeast Ohio, at the foothills near the panhandle of West Virginia. He counts money until his fingers bleed at a gaming resort, and lives with his dog, Jack. His stories have been published on the webzines Lucrezia Magazine, The Green Muse, Wild Violet Magazine, Anotherealm, Astoundingtales, Afterburn SF, Demon Minds, Bent, Lunatic Chameleon, Justus Roux, Logical Lust, Ruthie's Club and Forbidden Fruit Magazine; and they have been included in the erotic anthologies *Just the Sex, My First Time 3, Treasure Trail, Ultimate Gay Erotica 2008* and *Justus Roux's Erotic Tales 2*. He has stories in print in *Sofa Ink Quarterly, First Hand LTD, Writer's Post Journal, Mandate, Playguy, Torso, Men Magazine* and *Adventures for the Average Woman*.

DALE CHASE has been happily writing male erotica for a decade, with more than one hundred stories published in various magazines and anthologies, including translation into German and Italian. Her single nonerotic effort was published in the *Harrington Gay Men's Fiction Quarterly*. Chase is currently working on a collection of ghostly male erotica as well as an erotic western novel. She is a California native and lives near San Francisco.

KAL COBALT cowrites a food blog and has written about sex amongst foodies before (in *Country Boys*), but has yet to stumble upon a hot chef in a dark alley. Other K.C. erotica can be found in *Best Fantastic Erotica* and *Best Gay Romance 2008*. Online, find Kal in Velvet Mafia, Clean Sheets and Fishnet. Kal's Circlet.com essay, "10 Things You Always Wanted to Know about Robot Sex," was recently featured on Susie Bright's blog. Kal is a news writer and feature author for *Reality Sandwich* (about consciousness, not food). Learn more or contact K.C. at kalcobalt.com.

TED CORNWELL is a poet, fiction writer and journalist who grew up in Minnesota and has lived in New York for the past decade. His fiction has appeared in *Dorm Porn* and *Best Gay Love Stories 2006: New York City* and his poetry has appeared in the queer journal *modern words*.

THOMAS FUCHS has spent much of his career writing television documentaries and some print nonfiction. Over the past few years, he has turned to writing fiction. He lives in West Hollywood and can be reached at fuchsfoxxx@cs.com.

DREW GUMMERSON was born in 1971 and lives in Leicester, England. In 2003, his debut novel, *The Lodger*, was a Lambda Literary Award finalist. His latest novel, *Me and Mickie James*, will be published by Jonathan Cape in Summer 2008. Visit him at www.drewgummerson.co.uk.

ARDEN HILL is an all-around queer with an MFA in creative writing from Hollins University. His primary partner and genre is poetry, though he enjoys encounters with erotica, creative nonfiction and the critical essay. He is a poetry editor for Breath and Shadow, an online journal of disability culture and literature. His erotica has appeared in *Best Gay Erotica 2008*, and his first book of poetry is forthcoming from Side Show Press.

PHILLIP MACKENZIE, JR. is a slacker in a postslacker world, eking out a living as a freelance writer from his tumbling down house on the east side of L.A. He has broken down in Burlington, North Carolina, but that's as far as the similarities to his story go.

SYD MCGINLEY is an expat Brit living in Ohio and corrupting young minds at a state university. Syd's work appeared in *Hot Gay Erotica*. Visit www.sydmcginley.com for more queer erotica.

KEITH PECK, a fanatically loyal servant to the evil Lord Xenu (or Xemu), is currently held captive, and called No. 6, by the rabid were-hillbillies of eastern Tennessee. He seeks escape. Sometimes he is an IPv4 packet, roaming the Internet, noncorporeal. Other times he lies on a cot in his cell, dreaming of Bondi and thinking of Adrian. But Rover, it seems, never sleeps.

CHRISTOPHER SCHMIDT's poetry and essays can be found in recent issues of *Tin House, Court Green, Canadian Poetry* and *BUTT* magazine. His first book of poems, *The Next in Line*, won the Slope Editions Book Prize, selected by Timothy Liu. He writes a blog at http://www.thenextinline.com.

J. M. SNYDER writes gay erotic/romantic fiction. Originally self-published, Snyder now works with e-publishers Amber Quill, Aspen Mountain and Torquere Presses. Snyder's short gay fiction has been published online at Ruthie's Club, Tit-Elation and Amazon Shorts, as well as in anthologies published by Cleis Press and Alyson Books. A full bibliography, as well as free stories, excerpts, purchasing info and contests, can be found on the author's website at http://jmsnyder.net.

ANDREW WARBURTON is a PhD student specializing in literary theory. Until recently he worked as a copywriter, research assistant, and reporter in London, but has moved to the United States to continue his studies. His short stories have appeared in *Best Gay Bondage Erotica* and *Hustlers: Erotic Stories of Sex for Hire*, and his poetry has appeared in the queer literary journal *Chroma*.

CLARENCE WONG writes fiction depicting culture collisions: gay men navigating in a straight world, Asian immigrants transplanted to a Western society. His work has been published in the *Harrington Gay Men's Fiction Quarterly* and *Silver Kris*, the in-flight magazine of Singapore Airlines. A graduate of Princeton and Stanford universities, he believes in the transformative power of a good story. He lives in San Francisco.

ABOUT THE EDITOR

RICHARD LABONTÉ has edited the *Best Gay Erotica* series since 1997. He writes the occasional newsletter, *Books to Watch Out For*, and the fortnightly book review column, "Book Marks," distributed by Q Syndicate. With Lawrence Schimel, he is coeditor of *The Future is Queer* and *First Person Queer*, for Arsenal Pulp Press. He has edited *Hot Gay Erotica*, *Country Boys*, *Best Gay Romance 2008* and *Where the Boys Are* for Cleis Press, where he is also an editor at large. He lives mostly on Bowen Island, British Columbia, a stone's throw from the Pacific Ocean, and sometimes on a farm in rural eastern Ontario, surrounded by two hundred acres of hay.